MY FAMILY AND OTHER GHOSTS

MY FAMILY
AND OTHER GHOSTS

LOU KUENZLER

ILLUSTRATED BY STEVE BROWN

SCHOLASTIC

Scholastic Children's Books
An imprint of Scholastic Ltd
Euston House, 24 Eversholt Street, London, NW1 1DB, UK
Registered office: Westfield Road, Southam, Warwickshire, CV47 0RA
SCHOLASTIC and associated logos are trademarks and/or
registered trademarks of Scholastic Inc.

First published in the UK by Scholastic Ltd, 2019

Text copyright © Lou Kuenzler, 2019

The right of Lou Kuenzler to be identified as
the author of this work has been asserted.

ISBN 978 1407 17841 7

A CIP catalogue record for this book
is available from the British Library.

Printed by CPI Group (UK) Ltd, Croydon, CR0 4YY
Papers used by Scholastic Children's Books are made
from wood grown in sustainable forests.

1 3 5 7 9 10 8 6 4 2

www.scholastic.co.uk

To my family and other friends.

– Lou K

CHAPTER ONE: A DARK AND STORMY NIGHT

It was a dark and stormy night ... and Ivy Graves woke to see a shadowy face staring in through her bedroom window.

"Oh my goodness!" she gasped. "It's Grandpa Digby!"

There were three reasons why Ivy was so surprised:

One: She had never met her Grandpa Digby before. (She only really recognized him by the bushy grey eyebrows she'd seen in the faded photo of him in the living room.)

1

Two: Ivy's bedroom was on the eighteenth floor of a tower block (and there was no balcony outside to stand on – not even a proper windowsill, really).

Three (and perhaps most surprising of all): Grandpa Digby was dead.

He was very dead. Or, at least, he was *supposed* to be.

Grandpa Digby had died ten-and-a-half years ago, on the very same day that Ivy was born. Just as she had come into the world, poor old Grandpa Digby had left it. Ivy had always imagined it being a bit like those swirly doors you see in posh hotels. One person comes in, then the revolving door spins round, and another person goes out. Except, in Ivy's case, there'd been two of them arriving – because Ivy shared her birthday with her twin brother, Ash. Her *younger* twin, born twenty-two minutes after her (as she never tired of telling him). They had both been born on the same day that poor old Grandpa Digby had packed his mortal suitcase and checked out of the Land Of The Living Hotel.

"Yikes!" cried Ash, sitting up in bed suddenly and banging his head on the bottom of Ivy's bunk above him. "Did you see that? I saw a face at the window! A strange, shadowy face with HUGE bushy eyebrows. But ... but ... we're eighteen floors off the ground and there isn't even a—"

"Balcony," said Ivy, finishing Ash's sentence. She did that a lot. "It's a ghost," she added calmly. "He's floating."

"A ... g-g-ghost?" Ash made a sound like a gulping goldfish, as the face bobbed past the glass.

"Don't you recognize him?" Ivy jumped down from the top bunk. "It's Grandpa Digby," she said, padding to the window. "We'd better see what he wants."

"Don't!" cried Ash, as lightning flashed across the stormy sky.

Ivy ignored him. She did that a lot, too.

She calmly pushed up the catch and opened the window as far as it would go – which was about the width of a jam sandwich. All the windows, in all the flats on the eighteenth floor, only opened to a standard sandwich thickness. It was to stop anything thicker than a sandwich from falling out.

"Hello, Grandpa Digby! Nice to meet you," she said, peering through the gap. "Sorry." She gave the window another shove. "That's the best I can manage, I'm afraid."

4

"No bother, lass. Nice to meet you too," said Grandpa Digby's ghost. He had a thick, dusty voice, as if his throat was full of cobwebs. He floated closer to the window. "This'll do nicely."

"Of course!" said Ivy, jumping up and down excitedly. "I bet you can walk through walls and windows and things, can't you? I mean, you *are* a ghost..." She trailed off, wondering if it was rude to mention that sort of thing. Perhaps spooks didn't like being reminded that they were D-E-A-D. But Grandpa Digby just chuckled and gave a musty cough, as the storm jostled him about.

"Psst," hissed Ash, tugging at the sleeve of Ivy's pyjamas. "Psst ... Ivy." She ignored him (again).

"Actually, I'm not so good at the whole walking-through-walls thing," admitted

Grandpa Digby, still floating outside the window and shouting a little to be heard over the wind. "I have a tendency to get stuck halfway through. I once spent six whole weeks wedged sideways in the plaster between the library and the ballroom at Grave Grange."

"Library?" said Ivy. "Ballroom?" She'd imagined poor Grandpa Digby lying quietly in the cemetery ever since he had passed away. But it was obvious now that this stormy night wasn't the first time he'd been up and about. "Where's Grave Grange?" she asked.

Grandpa Digby didn't seem to hear her – or perhaps he was ignoring her. Ivy didn't like being ignored.

"Where's Grave Grange?" she repeated, shouting a little too loudly so that Grandpa Digby would be sure to hear her above the wind. But he still didn't answer the question.

"You should meet my friend Harold the Headless Huntsman," he said, wagging a shadowy finger. "Now, he's an expert wall-walker. So he should be, mind you. He's had almost four hundred years to practise."

"Four hundred years?" said Ivy. "You know people who have been dead for *four hundred years*?" This was so exciting, she couldn't bear it.

"Aghhh!" Ash did not sound excited. He made a strangled sound like a python might if you tied it in a knot. "D-did you say *Headless* Huntsman?"

"Pah! He's a rotten old show-off, that's what he is." Grandpa Digby waved his hand dismissively. "I'll tell you what, though, I'm not a bad slider myself. Not once I put my mind to it." He floated right up to the glass and peered through the sandwich-sized slit.

"Yes. I should manage that, no problem."

"A slider?" said Ivy. "Do you mean ... you're going to try and slip through that tiny gap in the window?"

"It would certainly be easier than having to hold our conversation from out here," said Grandpa Digby, a little crossly. "All this floating about plays havoc with my dodgy hip."

"Oh!" Ivy had never imagined that floating might be hard work but, as she peered out into the darkness, she could see the old ghost's legs were churning up and down in mid-air as if he was pedalling an invisible bicycle. "Sorry," she said, stepping back to make room. "How very rude of us, Grandpa Digby. Do come—"

"No!" Ash leapt between her and the window. "What are you doing, Ivy? Are you mad?" he asked. "NEVER invite a

8

ghost into your home."

"Actually, that's vampires," said Grandpa Digby, calmly sliding over the window-frame like a misty dishcloth. "You're quite right, lad, NEVER invite a vampire into your home. But I'm afraid to say, ghosts can come in whether we're invited or not."

The foggy dishcloth rearranged itself into a Grandpa Digby shape again, as he stood in front of them on the carpet.

Close up, under the electric light of the bedroom, Ivy saw that his ghostly skin was not a rich, dark brown colour (like the photograph of Grandpa Digby in the living room). Instead, his shadowy outline had a sort of blue-ish tinge. His feet were the shadowiest of all, melting into bluey-grey mist where they touched the floor.

"Hello!" he said, patting each of the twins on the head.

"Brrr!" Ivy giggled. "That's cold!" It was as if she had been touched by a snowman.

"Yikes!" Ash leapt in the air

"Sorry! We ghosts tend to be a bit chilly." Grandpa Digby smiled. "I hope I haven't given you the heebie-jeebies, turning up like this," he said. "I expect I do look a bit of a fright."

The old ghost glanced towards the full-length mirror on their wardrobe door.

"Oh, dear me," he chuckled.

His baggy shirt, jacket and trousers were dusty grey and a cobweb poked from his top pocket like a forgotten handkerchief.

"We're just glad you came," said Ivy, stepping closer and looking into the mirror too. Although Ash was still hanging back, cowering in background, she could see all three of their reflections framed together – like a spooky selfie with Grandpa Digby in the middle.

Ivy spotted the family resemblance right away.

We've all got slightly sticky-out ears, she thought with a giggle, although Ash and Grandpa Digby's were more noticeable. Hers were hidden by her shoulder-length curly hair.

The twins both had dark brown hair. Grandpa Digby's was dusty grey, but funny little tufts stuck up on the top in exactly the same way that Ash's always did.

What Ivy noticed most was that all three of them had identical big brown eyes. Beneath his bushy grey eyebrows, Grandpa Digby's still twinkled brightly, bringing a glow of warm light to his shadowy face.

"Wow!" Ivy gasped. "This is so cool!"

"Wrong," whimpered Ash. His hand shot out towards the dressing table and he grabbed the old baseball cap he always wore and rammed it on to his head, pulling it right down over his own big sparkly eyes as usual. "This is *not* cool at all," he mumbled. "It's creepy ... and weird ... and *supernatural*."

"Ash!" Ivy kicked him in the shins (a little harder than she meant to).

"Don't be so rude," she hissed. She knew he was shy, but that was no excuse. Not when a real live ghost (or a real *dead* one) had come all this way to visit them from beyond the grave, and on such a terrible night too.

"How about a nice, warm cup of tea?" she asked. Old people love tea. The least she could do was offer Grandpa Digby some. "We've got biscuits, too," she added encouragingly. "Dad baked them. So they might be a little unusual, but. . ." Ivy paused, wondering if ghosts could eat or drink anything at all once they were no longer *A-L-I-V-E*.

"Or I could wake Dad up for you, if you like," she said, remembering he was Grandpa Digby's son. Dad had raised the

13

twins on their own, ever since their mum had left when they were babies. He was the best dad in the world, but he'd been very glum lately – especially after losing his job as the chef in a local burger bar (his "experimental" custard-flavoured mustard had not been a good idea). Ivy thought it might cheer Dad up to be reunited with his long-lost father from beyond the grave.

But Grandpa Digby shook his head. "Best not. It's you youngsters I've come to see. I have something important to tell you," he said in a ghostly whisper. Something which could change your lives – and my afterlife – for ever!"

"What is it?" Ash whimpered, sounding like he'd rather stand barefoot on the prongs of a plug than hear the answer.

"Tell us," begged Ivy, almost exploding with excitement.

"I want you two and your dad to come and live with me," said Grandpa Digby simply. "At Grave Grange."

"Wicked!" cried Ivy, feeling at once that living with a ghost was definitely going to be exciting. "But you still haven't told us: where is Grave Grange exactly?"

"Ah!" said Grandpa Digby, with a slow smile. "The real question is *what* is Grave Grange?"

"Well? Go on!" Ivy couldn't bear the suspense a moment longer. She tried to grab at Grandpa Digby's sleeve, but her fingers passed right through as if she was touching a spider's web. "Tell us everything!"

"Grave Grange is a hotel," he explained at last, "in a big, old house, on a big, old hill."

"A big, old, *haunted* house?" Ash shuddered nervously.

Ivy, meanwhile, was leaping up and down in the air, clapping her hands. At last, a REAL adventure! "I've never even stayed in a hotel, let alone lived in one," she blurted out.

"Then you're in for a treat!" Grandpa Digby's eyes twinkled beneath his huge grey eyebrows.

"What Grave Grange needs," he explained, "is a new head chef – the sort of person who could be his own boss, and run the hotel too." Grandpa Digby waved a rolled-up scroll in the air. "All the details are here."

"A head chef? That would suit Dad perfectly. It's his dream job," cried Ivy, thinking how wonderful it would be to live in a hotel – and with Grandpa Digby, too. She took the scroll and thrust it into Ash's hands. She knew he'd be interested in double-checking all the tiny details, but she didn't care. All she knew was that it was a brilliant idea.

"Dad loves cooking," she beamed.

"But we can't run a hotel," said Ash quietly.

"Of course you can. I'll be there to help," promised Grandpa Digby. He was already slipping back over the windowsill. "All you have to do is convince your dad that the move is a good idea. Although ... perhaps it might be best if you don't mention—"

"Ghosts?" said Ash. "Visits from dead people?"

"Exactly! That's the spirit." The old ghost wagged a blurry finger at them from beyond the glass.

"Goodbye, Grandpa Digby," called Ivy, as his shimmering shape melted away into the dawn light. "We'll join you at Grave Grange as soon as we can, I promise."

CHAPTER TWO: THE ANCIENT YELLOW SCROLL

The ancient yellow scroll almost crumbled to dust in Ash's shaking fingers.

"Yikes," he said. "I don't like this one little bit."

There were three main reasons Ash wasn't keen on the scroll:

One: It looked scary (like the skin of an Ancient Egyptian mummy he had once seen in a museum).

Two: It smelt scary (like damp dungeons,

cobwebs and . . . well, a bit like the toilets at school).

Three (and most terrifying of all): It had been thrust into their hands by a ghost – so whatever was written inside was bound to be scary. (Very scary.)

"Can't we just throw it out of the window and forget anything ever happened?" asked Ash, peering into the pale dawn light, where Grandpa Digby's ghost had long since vanished.

"No!" said Ivy. "We can't." She folded her arms and glared at him. "Grandpa Digby came all this way to visit us. He's come up with a brilliant plan to find a new job for Dad. The least we can do is read what the message says."

"Fine." Ash sighed. He peered out from under his cap and saw that Ivy's face was glowing. She was wrinkling her nose and her

19

big dark eyes were sparkling with excitement (bad signs). He knew it was useless to argue with her when she was like this. His twin sister was only twenty-two minutes older than him (as she never tired of telling Ash), but they both knew she was the boss by about twenty-two thousand light-years. Worse still, she was always on the lookout for adventure. Ash did not like adventure. Ash did not like change – not even rearranging his sock drawer. Yet here was Ivy, and the ghost of dead Grandpa Digby, trying to turn their whole life upside down.

"Just remember," he said, "whatever happens, it was your idea." Ash opened the scroll quickly (as if he was pulling off a plaster) so it would be over before he had any more time to worry.

CREAK! The paper made a high, whining sound as it unrolled, like the door of a haunted house blowing in the wind.

"Ahhhh!" Ash leapt backwards, dropping the scroll on the floor. They both stared down at the open page and read what it said:

Comme tommorrow!

"Come tomorrow?" said Ash. "Is that it?" Grandpa Digby had promised details. This was just two words scrawled in green ink, and whoever had written them couldn't even spell properly.

"There's an address too," said Ivy. "Look." She pointed to a smaller line scribbled at the bottom of the scroll.

Grave Grange, Darkmoor.

"Dartmoor!" said Ivy. "How lovely."

"No," Ash corrected her. "Not Dartmoor, Ivy. **Dark**moor." An address like that should be warning enough. It practically screamed STAY AWAY.

"Pity." Ivy shrugged. "They have really cute wild ponies on Dartmoor. Dad's friend Steve sent a postcard once."

"Yes," said Ash, "and I expect *Dark*moor has ponies, too. Headless ones that gallop around in the middle of the night!"

Even the thought of it made him shudder.

"Surely you don't really think we should all go and live in an actual haunted hotel, just because a ghost appeared and told us to," he said.

"Of course I do." Ivy yawned as she climbed into the top bunk. "He's not just any old ghost. He's our grandpa," she said. "And anyway, we don't know if Grave Grange is actually haunted."

"Yes we do," said Ash. "In case you've forgotten, Grandpa Digby lives there and he's—"

"Dead," agreed Ivy. "I suppose you've got a point."

"Not to mention his mate, Harry the Headless Huntsman," added Ash.

"Hmm." Ivy sounded thoughtful. For one, glorious minute Ash hoped that she might be about to change her mind over the whole moving-to-a-haunted-hotel-because-our-ghost-grandfather-asked-us-to thing.

"I'll admit, there is one problem," she said after a moment of silence.

"What is it?" Ash groaned. Was there some other terrible detail that he had missed?

"Dad will never agree to move house just because of a few scribbled words on an old scroll," said Ivy. "He won't even know about the job that Grandpa Digby promised. What we need is a proper advert giving all the details. On a website or something."

"And how exactly are we going to manage that?" asked Ash. But as soon as the words were out of his mouth, he knew what Ivy's answer was going to be.

"You can do it," she said brightly, hanging her head over the edge of the top bunk and grinning at him upside down like a happy (and very persuasive) bat. "You're brilliant at computers and that sort of thing. Come on, Ash. You know it's a good idea. The

job sounds perfect and Dad's been so miserable lately. Think what this fresh start would mean for him ... for us all? There are too many memories in this flat."

Ash knew exactly what Ivy was talking about.

"The toothbrush," he whispered, and Ivy nodded.

It was pink, worn-down and hidden in the back of the bathroom cupboard. Dad refused to throw it away. It had belonged to their mum.

Mum had left the family when the twins were still babies (on their first birthday, in fact). She had fallen in love with a long-distance lorry driver called Norman, and set off to the travel the world. They hadn't seen or heard from her since, except the occasional card on their birthday, or at Christmas.

"It's all right for us," said Ivy. "We never really knew her. But it's different for Dad. Everything reminds him of Mum. Even the wallpaper she chose in the living room, and the kitchen plates."

"And that toothbrush," said Ash. He had seen Dad just staring into the bathroom cupboard for what seemed like hours. Especially lately, now he had no job to go to.

"He needs to accept it," said Ivy. "Mum's not coming back."

"Not ever," agreed Ash. He knew it was true, though his tummy twisted like a bag of snakes just saying it.

"We have to get Dad out of here," said Ivy. "We have to help him move on with his life."

"But what about us?" said Ash weakly. "We can't just go running off... I've got an overdue library book to return. And we've got—"

"School to think about," said Ivy, finishing his sentence as usual. "Not after today, we haven't; it's the last day of term. Tomorrow will be the summer holidays." (She was completely ignoring the issue of the library book.)

"Fine!" Ash knew when he was beaten. "If you really think it'll make Dad happy, I suppose I could design an advert on the computer." He hugged his knees, rocking slightly, and began muttering his seventeen times table under his breath to try and calm his nerves.

"Brilliant! I knew I could rely on you. You're a hero!" Ivy beamed.

"No I'm not." Ash blushed. Heroes were brave and fearless. Heroes were not afraid of ghosts.

Ash was afraid of ghosts. Very, *very* afraid of ghosts.

"Seventeen times seventeen is two hundred and eighty nine," he mumbled.

It did not make him feel any better.

CHAPTER THREE: THE WORLD IS JUST NOT READY FOR BRUSSELS SPROUT BISCUITS

"The world is just not ready for Brussels sprout biscuits," said Dad, staring down at a plate of bright green cookies, covered in a layer of sparkly emerald glitter, and something small and white, which might have been coconut flakes (or maybe garlic).

"I'm sure they're delicious," said Ivy encouragingly – though she wasn't prepared to actually try one. "You're a great cook,

Dad. Very ... er ... cutting-edge. You know, experimental."

"Maybe that's the problem," said Dad. "Perhaps that's why I can't find a job. I've worked for just about every cafe owner in this town and they're just not ready for *experimental*."

"Exactly!" cried Ivy, seizing the chance to bring up the new job at Grave Grange. Across the table from her, Ash was being no help at all. He was hiding under his cap, as usual, looking worried.

"What you need is a restaurant of your own," said Ivy. "One in a hotel, maybe."

She sat back and smiled triumphantly, hoping that Dad would pick up on the idea.

But he just stared glumly at his untouched mug of morning tea. "Even when I do get a job, I can't keep it. There was the mustard–custard incident at the burger bar, of course. And do you remember Dolly's Diner?"

Ivy nodded. (It turned out that Dolly's Diner didn't actually belong to someone called Dolly at all – it was a tall, bald man called Ian with a moustache.) Dad hadn't even made it past the first breakfast order before Ian had fired him.

"All because I tried something new and added pickles to the blueberry pancakes," Dad groaned.

"What you need is people who will actually appreciate your food," said Ivy. "The sort of person who eats out at expensive restaurants and hotels. They love trying new dishes." She picked up the smallest of the bright green Brussels sprout biscuits and nibbled the edge to show her support. She only took a tiny, tiny bite – more like a lick, really. Ivy had been caught out by Dad's more experimental recipes before. Sardine milkshake was not something she'd forget in a hurry. Not to mention the liquorice Bolognese and vinegar ice cream. But the biscuits really didn't taste that bad — she was almost certain that was coconut on top.

"Delicious!" She took another bite. A bigger one. No. She was wrong. They did taste bad. *Really* bad.

There were three reasons the Brussels sprout biscuits tasted so disgusting:

One: They were made from Brussels sprouts.

Two: The little white flakes on top were not coconut.

Three: The little white flakes on top were not even garlic. (They were squid. Cold, wet, fish-flavoured squid on a Brussels sprout biscuit!)

Ivy slipped the biscuit back on her plate and tried to hide it under a slice of toast.

Dad didn't even notice. He just kept staring at his untouched cup of tea.

"What you need," said Ivy dramatically, "is a change."

"Change?" said Dad dully. "Even if I do get a job, most of the places around here won't even let me change my greasy apron. Let alone the menu."

"Maybe it's time for you to move on, then," said Ivy, kicking Ash under the table. Why was he just sitting there like a terrified teabag about to be dunked in a pot of boiling water? Surely he knew this was his cue?

"Oh, yes!" Ash pushed their ancient family laptop forward and turned the screen around to face Dad. "I was . . . er . . . just-browsing-online-this-morning. . ." he said in great nervous rush.

33

"And-I-happened-to-find-this." He really was a hopeless liar.

"It's an advertisement," finished Ivy, in her best grown-up voice, giving Ash a quick thumbs up. He might not be any good at fibbing, but he had done a great job of designing a pretend website and making the online advert look really official. He was brilliant at stuff like that. He'd even checked her spelling.

www.jobs-for-people-who-need-a-change.com
WANTED: Experimental chef to run spectacular hotel and restaurant. Must be happy to work alone and have flair for unusual cooking. All accommodation provided on site at our charming hotel: Grave Grange, Darkmoor.

Ivy held her breath as Dad read the advert.

"Flair for unusual cooking?" he said, after a pause which seemed to last for ever.

"Yes!" Ivy beamed. She was particularly proud of that line.

"And on Dartmoor?" said Dad, seeming at least a little bit interested. "That sounds nice. My friend Steve sent a postcard from Dartmoor once." He glanced over his shoulder as if checking to see whether it was still stuck on the fridge. "It had a picture of some really cute little ponies."

"No, Dad. Not *Dart*moor," said Ash. "*Dark*mo—"

Ivy kicked him under the table again. Hard.

"Don't you see, Dad? It would be the perfect job for you," she said. "You could plan your own brilliant menus for the restaurant. And you wouldn't have to have a boss or anything. The whole hotel would be yours!"

She saw that Dad was actually leaning forward to read the advert again. She looked over at Ash and grinned.

"I say!" Dad gulped a mouthful of his cold tea. "It does sound jolly interesting." There was a spark of energy in his voice that Ivy hadn't heard for months.

"We could all live there together, out in the countryside," she said.

"With dead Grandpa Digby," muttered Ash.

Ivy narrowed her eyes at him.

"It'll be a big adventure, Dad. Go on," she urged. "All you have to do is apply."

"Hmm. . ." Dad scratched his chin.

Ivy sat very still, hoping as hard as she could that he'd say yes. Ash fidgeted nervously.

"Well. . ." (Another dreadful pause.)

"I suppose it's worth a shot," said Dad finally. "The place is called Grave Grange, after all. That's almost the same as our family name."

"The Graves of Grave Grange! See? It's made for us," cried Ivy.

A huge smile spread across her face. It had taken a ghostly visit from their long-dead grandfather, and all the cunning she and Ash could muster, but it seemed like they might have managed to get Dad excited about something again, at long last.

"Grave Grange, here we come," she whispered, crossing her fingers for good luck.

CHAPTER FOUR: TURN AROUND WHEN POSSIBLE

"Turn around," screamed the satnav. "Turn around when possible." The machine's normally calm voice was quaking with fear.

"I think we ought to listen," said Ash. But it was too late, Ivy was leaning her head right out of the car window even though it was pouring with rain.

"Look. There's a sign," she cried, bouncing up and down in the front passenger seat.

Their poor little car was crammed to

the roof with weird-looking cooking utensils, and bags and boxes full of their possessions. Ash was hunched up in the back next to Dad's pots, pans and mixing machines. A potato masher was digging into his side.

"See?" Ivy pointed at something through the downpour.

She was right. There was a sign. A twisted metal post with a single arrow, like a crooked finger pointing out across the windswept moors.

GRAVE GRANGE:

ONE MILE. ABANDON HOPE
ALL YE WHO ENTER HERE

"I *definitely* think we should turn around now," said Ash. But nobody took the slightest notice.

Dad was singing along in time to the swoosh of the windscreen wipers. Singing! Actually *singing*! Ash had barely seen Dad smile since Christmas, and now here he was belting out the words to Elvis Presley's "Heartbreak Hotel".

Ash knew there were three things Dad really loved in the world:

One: The twins, of course (which was lucky as he was their dad).

Two: Cooking. (The more wild and wacky the recipe, the better.)

Three: Elvis Presley. (The King of Rock 'n' Roll.)

It had been ages since Ash had heard Dad sing like this, though. Perhaps Ivy

was right – this new job really did cheer him up.

"Don't worry, son. I'm sure that old sign is only a joke," he said, turning left and following the arrow through a deep puddle.

Ash pulled his cap down and held on tight as they bumped on over a potholed track.

"I can't let the nice people at Grave Grange down," said Dad seriously. "They accepted my application so quickly. They seem dead keen to take me on."

"Exactly!" Ash gulped. "*Dead* keen. That's what I'm worried about."

Ivy spun round in the front seat and gave him a hard stare. (**Really** hard).

It was the twins themselves, of course, who had replied to Dad's job application on the fake website they had built. Now,

Ash wished with every tingling nerve in his body that they had turned Dad down.

"There it is!" cried Ivy, sticking her head out of the window again and pointing through the rain. "There's Grave Grange. Do you see it?"

"No!" Ash closed his eyes and screwed them tight shut. "I don't see anything."

He couldn't even bear to look.

CHAPTER FIVE: HIGH ON THE WINDY MOOR

High on the windy moor stood Grave Grange.

"Wow!" For once, Ivy was almost lost for words. *Almost*. "Wow," she said again. "Wowzer wow wow!"

As the car began to climb the steep hill, she saw that the old, tumbledown hotel was even weirder and spookier than she could ever have hoped for.

"Isn't it perfect?!" she cried.

The sooty-grey brickwork was hung with

thick black creepers and vines, tumbling over iron-fringed balconies, while gargoyles with the heads of dragons spat rainwater on to the cobbles below. Far above, turrets, towers and turnip-topped domes rose out of the towering rooftops. Everything about the strange pointy building looked wonderfully old, dark and mysterious.

It wasn't a castle, exactly. It was more ... jumbled-up than that. As Ivy stared hard at the higgledy-piggledy shape, she could see, right in the middle, what might once have been a large, square-looking house. It was as if a child with thick black felt-tip pen had got bored and started doodling – adding battlements and chimneys, nooks and crannies, columns and curly bits, and even a huge drawbridge over a little moat at the front.

"Crikey," said Dad. "Golly-gosh."

"Gaaa," said Ash. Ivy peered round at her brother cowering amongst the piles of pots and pans on the back seat. His cap was pulled right down over his face, but she knew that his eyes would be closed too.

"It'll be all right," she whispered. "You'll see." After all, Grandpa Digby would be there to help them.

Their little car spluttered and juddered like a cat with a furball as it tried to climb up the last twisting stretch of bumpy driveway to the top of the steep hill.

"I just hope there are some guests," said Dad. "Hotels need three things to survive."

He listed what those three things were:

One: Guests.

Two: Guests.

Three: More guests.

"If there aren't any guests, there won't

be any money to pay my wages or settle the bills," said Dad. "If there aren't any guests, we'll be heading home before the month is over."

"There'll be guests," said Ivy confidently. But she wasn't at all sure it was true.

The car crawled forward, groaning under the weight of all the bags and boxes they had crammed in when they'd packed up their belongings from the flat. Their kitchen table, an armchair and Dad's bread-making machine were tied to the roof. Ivy couldn't stand it – they were driving so slowly she could imagine snails overtaking them.

"Can I get out and run on ahead?" she asked.

"I don't see why not," said Dad, as the car stalled completely. They ground to a halt in front of a huge iron sign by the gates:

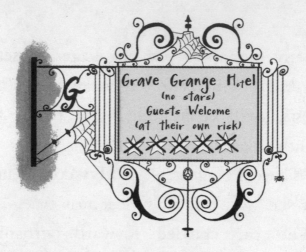

As Ivy heaved a pile of cookery books off her knees, she saw that the rain had stopped. Pale streaks of golden-yellow sun were glistening through the dark clouds.

"See?" she said, kneeling on her seat and smiling over at Ash who was peeping out from under the brim of his cap at last. "I told you it would be all right."

"How about it, son? Do you want to go on ahead with your sister, too," asked Dad.

"Gaa!" said Ash again, which Ivy took to mean no.

"See you later, then." She leapt out of the car and slammed the door before a stack of dinner plates could fall out.

"If there's anyone at reception, tell them we're on our way," said Dad, a little uncertainly. "Just don't climb on anything. I'm not sure it looks very safe."

"It isn't!" said Ash.

But Ivy was already charging up the steep, twisting driveway, towards the huge open drawbridge in the distance and the shadowy courtyard beyond.

CHAPTER SIX: RUN!

"Run!" said the satnav. "Abandon your vehicle and run for your lives!"

"I think something's gone wrong with that thing." Dad chuckled.

"I really think we should listen to it!" said Ash.

But Dad was too busy trying to restart the car and muttering about a new menu featuring "Grave Grange gravy with fish".

Ash winced as the engine finally sprung into life and they drove on up the hill towards the hotel.

"Seventeen times seventeen is two hundred and eighty-nine," Ash chanted under his breath.

It *still* didn't make him feel any better.

CHAPTER SEVEN: IS ANYBODY THERE?

"Hello!" called Ivy. "Is anybody there?"

She jumped as a strange thumping sound came from somewhere in the wall behind her.

Probably just the pipes, she thought. Old buildings like this always had trouble with their pipes.

"Hello?" she called again. The drawbridge had been down, so she had just walked straight in, but there didn't seem to be a soul about. The huge reception hall was so empty only her own voice came echoing back to her ... and another dull thud from the wall.

Ivy shivered. *I hope those rumbling pipes don't mean the heating's busted*, she thought. It was so cold in the huge stone hall, it was like standing in a fridge.

She thrust her freezing hands into her pockets and strode over to the reception desk. There was a notice in a dusty frame. Ivy blew away the cobwebs and read:

WELCOME TO
GRAVE GRANGE HOTEL

ROOMS AVAILABLE:
FOR ONE NIGHT
FOR ONE WEEK
FOR ALL ETERNITY

Well, at least that means they're open, thought Ivy. She rang the little silver bell next to the frame.

Ping!

Ivy didn't quite know what she was expecting, but she'd hoped that Grandpa Digby might be here to meet them. Then she noticed the thick flecks of dust dancing in a shaft of pale sunlight glinting through the arrow slit above her head. She remembered it was only the middle of the afternoon and still light outside. Perhaps ghosts didn't appear in the daytime . . . but what about living people? Were there any of those here?

Maths wasn't Ivy's strong point, but even she knew Dad was right. You needed money to make a business work. And in the hotel *business,* guests meant money. They'd definitely need a few of those if this was going to be Dad's new job.

BAM!

Ivy stumbled forward as something hit her on the back of her head.

"Ouch!" She spun around. "What was that?"

SLAM!

Something hit her on the nose.

"Stop it!" Ivy ducked.

WHAM!

Something hit her on the bum.

"What's happening?" cried Ivy. Old books and candlesticks were flying through the air towards her. A tinkling laugh echoed round the hall, but Ivy still couldn't see anybody.

Was this a guest? Ivy had always thought that the sort of people who stay in hotels would be posh and well-behaved.

"I've had enough of this!" she cried, as a wastepaper basket shaped like an elephant's foot flew past her left ear. "Whoever you are, come out and show yourself."

There were three things confusing Ivy as she skidded under the reception desk to take cover:

One: *Who* was doing this?

Two: *How* were they doing it?

Three: *Why* were they doing it?

"I'm sorry if I've upset you somehow. I don't mean any harm," she said, poking her head out from behind the table leg and talking to the empty room. "My name is Ivy."

PING!

The little silver bell shot off the top of the desk above her, only missing her nose by a millimetre.

"I'm Digby's granddaughter," explained Ivy, retreating. "Digby Graves. Do you know him?" She had a clear view from under all sides of the desk and couldn't see anyone's legs anywhere near it. That meant no one could have got close enough to throw the bell ... not unless they were invisible. "Are you a ghost?" asked Ivy.

"Certainly not!" said a squeaky voice. Then there was a long rude sound like somebody blowing a raspberry. "I'm a poltergeist, silly!"

"Really? How interesting." Ivy was delighted. "I've always wanted to meet one of those." She knew poltergeists were a sort of naughty spook who liked to throw things around.

Cautiously, she stuck her head out from under the table again. Although the stone floor was strewn with debris, nothing was flying through the air any more.

A door at the far side of the hall swung open, and the tinkly laugh faded away.

"Wait!" Ivy leapt to her feet. "Come back." The voice had sounded like it belonged to a young girl. "We could be friends if you like."

"Ha!" The poltergeist blew another loud raspberry. "If you want to play with me, you'll have to find me first." Her high voice echoed back along the corridor.

BOOM!

The heavy wooden door slammed shut in Ivy's face.

CHAPTER EIGHT: EVERYTHING WILL BE ALL RIGHT

"Everything will be all right," Ash told himself, as he stepped into the huge entrance hall at Grave Grange. He was carrying a pile of saucepans that Dad had asked him to take down to the big kitchen in the basement.

They'd finally parked their car outside the hotel, and had a chance to look around a bit. Although the ancient building was definitely old and creepy and very dusty, Ash hadn't seen anything too terrible yet.

(Although he could have sworn the fishy eyes of the stuffed salmon in the glass case on the mantelpiece were following him across the room).

Other than a dead fish, there didn't seem to be anyone else  here at all. No guests. No staff. And no sign of Ivy anywhere. She had disappeared completely.

Typical! Ash thought.

There was no sign of Grandpa Digby either, even though the old ghost had promised he would be there to help them.

Ash jumped as something in the wall behind him made a heavy thumping sound.

"Don't panic. It's probably only the pipes," he whispered under his breath. "Seventeen times twenty eight is four hundred and seventy-six."

Ash tried to stay calm. He swallowed hard.

"I don't mind what happens," he reassured himself. "Just as long as I don't meet that hideous headless huntsman Grandpa Digby told us about..."

CHAPTER NINE: PLAYING WITH A POLTERGEIST

Playing with a poltergeist was much harder work than Ivy had imagined.

There were three things which made the game of hide and seek especially tricky:

One: The poltergeist was invisible.

Two: The poltergeist kept throwing things.

Three: This particular poltergeist was a very good shot.

"Ouch!" cried Ivy, as a stuffed badger bounced off her shoulder and rolled away down the stairs. "Where are you even finding these things?"

"Serves you right!" There was a swish of tapestry curtains as the poltergeist seemed to rush past.

"Wait!" called Ivy. "You haven't seen my Grandpa Digby anywhere, have you? I ought to try and find him."

"No! Haven't seen him for days." The invisible poltergeist blew yet another raspberry and a door banged at the end of the long corridor (which Ivy guessed must mean she was all alone again and the poltergeist was gone).

"How strange," she muttered. Grandpa Digby had promised he would be here to meet them. What could have happened to him? Ivy had no idea how to run the hotel without his help.

She was just about to start exploring some

of the rooms up here, in case Grandpa Digby was wafting about in one of them, when she heard a blood-curdling scream coming from the floor below. (A scream she knew only too well.)

"Ash," she cried, turning on her heel and charging down the stairs as fast as her legs would carry her. "Ash? Where are you?"

CHAPTER TEN: THERE'S NOTHING AS FRIGHTENING AS A HEADLESS HUNTSMAN

"There's nothing as frightening as a headless huntsman..." Ash kept telling himself. As long as he didn't meet the decapitated spook, he might just about be able to cope.

But that was before he heard the voices.

"Hello, dearie."

"Hello, dear."

"Hello."

It was like an echo — a soft, whispering echo.

Ash turned around. That was his big mistake. That's when he saw them...

There were three of them. Three grey ladies – hovering by the reception desk.

"AARRGH!" Ash dropped the pile of saucepans he was holding with a clatter.

Then everything went black.

CHAPTER ELEVEN: THREE GREY LADIES

Three grey ladies were leaning over Ash's body.

"Leave him alone," cried Ivy, as she skidded to a halt in the doorway. The trio of ancient figures turned towards her with pale, toothless grins.

Ivy's heart was pounding. This was all her fault. She was the one who had persuaded Ash it was a good idea to come here. Now he was lying flat on his back in the middle of the reception hall – saucepans scattered

all around him, his face as grey as cement –
while three menacing spirits bore down on
him from above.

"Ghosts!" he said, lifting his head and
whimpering. "They're ghosts, Ivy."

Ivy swallowed hard. She wasn't usually
afraid of anything – not when she'd seen
Grandpa Digby's face at the window in
the storm, or even when the invisible

poltergeist was throwing things at her. But these three hags were different. They seemed to have stepped out of the grave itself.

Then one of the grey ladies tutted.

"Ghosts?" she said. "Us?"

"Nonsense. We're the McEver Sisters," said the second grey lady.

"We live in the hotel," added the third.

"Oh!" Ivy gasped in surprise, as she realized how silly she had been. The grey figures weren't dead (at least, not yet), they were just very, very old ladies. She let out a great sigh of relief.

"You're guests, not ghosts," she cried in delight.

So there really were *real* people staying in the hotel after all — real people who could eat in Dad's restaurant! Although, the three grey McEver sisters looked so pale and serious she couldn't imagine their reaction to Dad's "experimental" cooking.

Ash sat up and pulled his cap back on to his head. "I think I must have fainted. Are you sure you're not..."

"Dead?" The first old lady tutted again. "How rude!"

"Certainly not," said the second.

"Although, I can see why you might think that," said the third one more kindly. "We are absolutely ancient." She giggled, and then all three McEver sisters began shaking from head to toe with laughter, their old bones rattling like coat hangers on a rail.

"Are they all right?" hissed Ash.

Ivy wasn't sure. But she was pleased the old ladies didn't look so stern any more.

"I'm Enid," wheezed the first one at last. "We're triplets."

"I'm Ethel," said the second. "We're a-hundred-and-three years old."

"I'm Edna. They're both older than me. I'm the youngest by a whole thirty minutes," said the third with a cheeky wink.

"That's amazing," cried Ivy. "We're twins. And I'm the oldest — by twenty-two minutes." She helped Ash shakily to his feet and they introduced themselves.

"Tell us, what brings youngsters like you to Grave Grange?" asked Enid.

"We haven't had any other guests here for years," agreed Ethel.

"Not a soul," added Edna.

"No other guests?" said Ivy, her heart sinking. "Oh dear." She wished Grandpa Digby would turn up and explain everything. How were they supposed to run a hotel if no new guests ever came?

"Now the manager's left too," said Edith

sadly.

"And the chef," added Ethel.

"I suppose the whole place will have to close down." Edna sighed.

The old ladies looked truly miserable at the thought of Grave Grange closing down.

"Don't worry," said Ivy encouragingly. "Everything is going to be all right. We're here to run the hotel. Our dad is the new manager and head chef all rolled into one."

"Oh, splendid. How lovely." The grey ladies grinned at Ivy, revealing rows of pink gums: they really didn't have a tooth between them.

"There's just one tiny problem," said (the one-who-Ivy-thought-might-be) Edith. It was hard to tell as the three elderly triplets were absolutely identical. They had switched places while they were speaking, so Ivy could only guess at who was who.

"We're so old, we've spent all our money," said (the-one-who–Ivy–thought-was) Ethel. "We can't afford to pay our bills anymore."

"I suppose you'll have to throw us out if we can't pay," said (the-one-who-might-be) Edna with a sigh. "That's what the old manager threatened to do before he left."

"Throw you out?" said Ivy. "Certainly not."

She tried not to catch Ash's eye. He'd most likely be thinking about maths and how they couldn't afford to let three old ladies stay in the hotel free of charge – not if they didn't have any other guests to help pay the bills. He'd be right, of course. But Ivy had taken to the three ancient sisters right away. She couldn't just turn them out on to the moor, especially not now the wind seemed to have picked up. She glanced through the open doorway and saw that it was raining again too.

Surely they would find some other guests for Grave Grange soon. Somehow...

"Don't you worry, the Graves family are here to look after you," she told the old ladies. They seemed so frail she felt as if they might fade away before her eyes. "Have you had anything to eat today?"

"Not a morsel," said (possibly) Ethel.

"Then Dad will make you something right away," said Ivy, spotting him struggling towards the drawbridge with a box of crockery under one arm, a herb rack under the other and a sieve on his head like a hat.

"I just hope you like unusual food," said Ash kindly. Ivy should have known he wouldn't be able to turn the old ladies out, any more than she would. "Only Dad's cooking can be a bit..."

"Experimental," said Ivy, finishing his

sentence for him.

"Oh, good," said the jolliest sister (who Ivy was fairly certain was Edna). "Experimental is my middle name."

"Nonsense!" said (possibly) Enid. "Your middle name is Maud."

Edna growled.

Ivy sensed an argument might be about to break out but, before things could get started, Dad reached the reception hall.

He was dripping wet. (His sieve-hat had done nothing to keep out the rain off, of course. It had dribbled straight through the holes.)

"Hello!" He smiled. "My name's Douglas. But You can call me Dug. Dug Graves. I'm the new ch—"

Unfortunately, at that moment, three things happened to Dad all at the same time:

One: He slipped backwards in a pool of

water from his own feet.

Two: He tripped over one of Ash's saucepans.

Three: The sieve on his head went flying through the air faster than a Frisbee thrown by a poltergeist.

"Look out," cried Ivy as the three old ladies ducked just in time.

"I'm so sorry," cried Dad, wobbling on one leg. His wet foot was still stuck in the saucepan and he was desperately clutching the box of crockery to his chest. The herb rack had been upended under his arm, and parsley, sage, rosemary and thyme were fluttering down to the floor like flakes of green snow. "Are you all right, ladies?" he gasped.

"Perfectly fine, thank you," said (almost certainly) Ethel grandly. Though she did look a little shaken after having nearly been decapitated by a flying sieve.

"Don't worry, Mr Graves," said (most likely) Edna reassuringly. "Things are always flying through the air around here."

"All the time," agreed (very probably) Enid. "It's just one of the hazards of staying at Grave Grange."

"Hazards?" asked Ash. "What do you mean, *hazards*?"

Nobody answered. Ivy wasn't surprised. The strange banging in the wall was so loud now, she could barely hear herself think.

"There we go!" shouted Dad, as he finally managed to pull his soggy foot out of the saucepan. He squelched forward to shake hands with each of the McEver sisters in turn. "I'm sure we can rustle up a delicious complimentary pudding to make up for your distress," he promised.

"As long as it's something nice and soft," said (might be) Ethel.

"Something easy to chew!" agreed (could be) Enid.

"We don't have many teeth left," explained (most definitely) Edna with a gummy grin.

"Blancmange!" cried Dad excitedly. "Or maybe a mousse ... a soufflé ... or perhaps a jelly?"

Ivy smiled. He was acting like a hotel chef already. (Even if the McEver Sisters were not actual *paying* guests.)

"Psst! Ivy." She felt Ash tugging at her sleeve. "Psst!" he whispered. "What do you think the Grey Ladies meant when they said things fly through the air all the time around here?"

"Erm... Maybe just that we have to be careful because floors are slippery, especially if they're wet," said Ivy, pointing down at the uneven flag stones.

This didn't seem like *quite* the right moment to tell her brother she had already met a poltergeist.

CHAPTER TWELVE: THERE REALLY *IS* NOTHING AS FRIGHTENING AS A HEADLESS HUNTSMAN

"There really is nothing as frightening as a headless huntsman..." Ash kept reassuring himself. As long as he didn't bump (head first) into the decapitated spook, everything else would be OK.

It was already the family's second evening at Grave Grange and, to Ash's surprise, only three really strange things had happened (so far):

One: The weird banging sound continued to come from the pipes in the reception hall.

Two: The fishy eyes of the huge stuffed salmon in the glass case were *definitely* following Ash around.

Three (and this one involved actual physical danger): A mysterious pot of flying marmalade (accompanied by a rude raspberry-blowing sound) had only narrowly missed hitting him as it whizzed past his ear at breakfast.

There was still no sign of Grandpa Digby anywhere, though, which did seem very odd, especially as he had promised he would be here to help them run the hotel.

It just proves, Ash thought, *that you should never trust a ghost. Not even one who is related to you.* Yet, he had to admit, life at the spooky hotel hadn't proved nearly as terrifying as he had feared. Right now, as the evening sun sank over the dark moors, Ash was acting as a waiter in the long, shadowy dining room.

"Delicious," said (probably) Edith, waving her spoon at him as she tucked into her pudding.

Strangely, the old grey ladies seemed to love Dad's cooking. As long as there was nothing chewy, he could be as experimental as he liked. His fizzy black squid-ink soup, followed by liquidized liver-and-lamb-chop mousse with baked bean purée, had gone down a storm, and the McEver sisters were just tucking into three bowls of his special cheesy-flavoured ice cream when (probably) Edna shivered.

"I say, young Ash." She smiled at him with a toothless grin. "This frozen dessert is making me chilly. You wouldn't be a dear and pop to the library for my shawl, would you? I left it there this afternoon."

"And my scarf," said (probably) Edith.

"And my sweater," begged (probably) Ethel.

"Erm. . ." Ash hesitated. He had popped his head around the door of the library earlier on that day – and popped it out again as fast as he could. It was a dark and gloomy-looking room full of cobwebs and huge black leather-bound books (nothing at all like the lovely, light, bright town library where he'd happily passed many hours researching things back home).

"Go on. Be a love."

"Be an angel."

"Be a sweetie."

A line of gummy grins beamed up at him.

"All right," said Ash. "I'll go." He had quickly grown fond of the grey McEver sisters (now that he knew they were real old ladies and not ghosts). It didn't seem fair that they should have to be cold just because he was afraid of a dusty old room full of books.

"I'll be as quick as I can," he said, hurrying towards the door. If Grave Grange was going to be his home (and it looked like it might be) he couldn't go on avoiding certain places just because they were dark or dingy. That would count out most of the rooms in the hotel.

"Where are you off to?" called Ivy as he sped across the reception hall (pursued by the swivelling eyes of the huge salmon

 in the glass case). Ivy was manning the reception desk, in the desperate hope that some new guests might miraculously check in.

"Library," he called back.

"Oh good. Are you going to work on publicity?" she asked. She had been pestering him all day to start an online campaign to promote Grave Grange. But Ash hadn't managed to find an internet connection in any of the rooms he had dared to visit so far.

"Just getting shawls 'n' things," he shouted over his shoulder, dashing on down the corridor and flinging open the door to the library before he could change his mind.

He was just bending down to pick up a

grey shawl from the arm of a big leather chair when he felt a cold draught blowing on the back of his neck.

"Brrr!" Ash rubbed his neck and turned around.

The first thing he saw was another neck – a neck belonging to somebody else.

"A-a—a-arrgh!"

Ash tried to scream, but the only sound that came out was a sort of strangled squeak.

The neck had no head attached to it... The (headless) neck was sticking out of the (headless) body of a small, round man dressed all in green.

"Yikes," Ash squeaked, "you're Harold the Headless Huntsman." Then his knees gave way beneath him.

CHAPTER THIRTEEN: IT'S PROBABLY BEST TO SKIP THIS ONE

It's probably best to skip this one. It's Chapter Thirteen … and thirteen is unlucky. Everybody knows that. (And poor Ash is in enough trouble as it is).

CHAPTER FOURTEEN: *PING!*

Ping!

The silver bell on the reception desk rang.

"Hello!" cried Ivy, jumping with surprise.

She looked up from the huge dusty visitor book she had been reading. According to the empty pages, no new guests had checked in to Grave Grange for twenty-five years. And even those guests were only the McEver sisters, who had clearly never left.

"Welcome..." she began, excited to see who had arrived at long last. But the hall was empty (except for the huge, grumpy stuffed fish glaring at her from the mantelpiece).

Ivy sighed. She had really hoped it might be some of the new guests Grave Grange so badly needed, but it was probably just the invisible poltergeist playing with the bell again. Then she noticed a thick leather glove lying on top of the reception desk.

"Excuse me?" she called. "Is anybody there?" Perhaps someone had passed through and left the glove while she was reading. But Ivy hadn't heard any of the various creaky doors leading off the hall being opened or closed.

"Hello?" she called again.

Other than the endless banging from the pipes, there was no reply.

"Strange," muttered Ivy, peering at the glove. It was made of brown leather and seemed far too big to belong to any of the three grey ladies. It didn't look like it would belong to Grandpa Digby either, Ivy realized with a pang. She desperately wished the old ghost would turn up and explain his plans in bringing them to Grave Grange.

But the glove looked too ancient even to belong to Grandpa Digby. There was something really old-fashioned about it. It was the sort of glove somebody might have worn if they were training a hawk or an owl. Ivy remembered a school trip they'd gone on once, to a big stately home in the middle of the countryside. There'd been a bird display at lunch while they ate their sandwiches. An eagle had tried to steal Ash's sausage-and-rice-pudding roll (one of Dad's more experimental packed lunches), until Ivy had waved her own mushroom-and-marmalade baguette in the air like a cudgel and frightened the bird away. (Ash wasn't very fond of eagles now.) (Or sausage-and-rice-pudding rolls.)

Smiling at the memory, Ivy leant forward to pick the glove up.

It was heavy. Much heavier than she would have expected.

"Odd!" Ivy peeped inside – and wished she hadn't. "Ew!"

Inside the glove was a hand. A real hand.

The hand was alive.
Or, at least, it was wriggling.

The glove leapt free of Ivy's grasp and  began to drum its fingers on the table.

"Can I help?" said Ivy politely. She supposed a receptionist at a hotel ought to be polite to anybody – even to a glove with a wriggly hand inside it. "Would you like a room for the night ... or just a cosy drawer to lie in, perhaps?"

The glove scuttled across the desk like a spider and picked up a sheet of old yellowy paper. Then it grabbed a feather-quill-pen from the end of the desk and wrote: **Greatings frome the Gory Glove**, in a familiar green scrawl.

"Of course!" cried Ivy in delight. "You wrote the scroll for us. That must mean you know Grandpa Digby. Do you have any idea where he is now?"

The glove tapped a finger impatiently on the yellow paper, and Ivy suddenly understood that it wanted her to write her question down.

She took the quill gently from its fingers and wrote in smudgy writing:

DO YOU KNOW WHERE GRANDPA DIGBY IS? HAVE YOU SEEN HIM SINCE HE BROUGHT US THE SCROLL?

The glove ran its fingers gently over the inky letters, as if feeling the wetness of their shape. Then it took the quill from Ivy and replied:

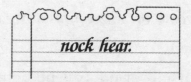

nock hear.

Ivy stared at the note in confusion. "Nock hear"? What could that mean? Then she remembered the wonky spelling on the scroll.

"*Not here*? Is that what you meant? Grandpa Digby hasn't come back?"

She sighed. Where could he be? Ivy thought of the vast lonely moors, and how windy it had been on the night that Grandpa Digby had visited them. The old spirit was only made of mist and air, it seemed. He could have been blown miles and miles off-course as he tried to return to Grave Grange through the storm.

"Oh, Grandpa Digby," she groaned. "Please hurry. Please find your way home."

As if in answer, there was a great crashing sound, louder even than the banging in the pipes, and the door that lead to the library was flung open.

"Hello?" cried Ivy, her heart leaping into her throat. "Grandpa Digby? Is that you?" Had he answered her call so quickly?

But she should have known from the sound of pounding feet that it wouldn't be the gentle old ghost of her grandfather who came wafting through the door. It was Ash – and he wasn't wafting at all. He was charging flat-out, fleeing with all the force of a wildebeest on the run.

CHAPTER FIFTEEN: YOU LOOK LIKE YOU'VE SEEN A GHOST

"You look like you've seen a ghost!" said Ivy as Ash stumbled into the hall.

Then she threw back her head and giggled at him. "I expect you probably have seen a ghost," she said. "This is a haunted hotel after all!"

Ash tried desperately to answer, but his voice was stuck somewhere deep inside his chest.

Ivy grabbed his sleeve. Her face was suddenly serious.

"It wasn't Grandpa Digby, was it?" she asked.

Ash shook his head. What he wanted to say was: *I just saw hideous Harold the horrible Headless Huntsman. He waggled his neck at me, then disappeared through the wall like green smoke.*

But it was no good.

Nothing came out.

Not a word.

Ash could see Ivy wasn't really listening any more anyway. She was waving a sheet of yellow paper at him. Meanwhile, a strange leathery glove seemed to be scuttling along the reception desk behind her. Scuttling ... all by itself.

"Isn't it brilliant? That's the Gory Glove," said Ivy, following his gaze. "It wrote the note for us on the scroll. But it doesn't seem to have seen Grandpa Digby since the night of the storm."

The glove snatched a piece of paper from a pile by the inkpot and scribbled something on it. Ash shrunk back as it leapt off the edge of the reception desk and scampered across the floor towards him. It ran on three fingers, holding the piece of yellow paper between its remaining finger and thumb like a crab's pinchers.

"Help!" cried Ash, finding his quavering voice again at last. The glove snatched hold of the hem of his trousers and started climbing up his leg. "Get off!" Ash tried to grab the glove and pull it away from his shins.

"I wouldn't look inside it, if I was you," warned Ivy.

Ash had no intention of looking inside the glove, of course. But as soon as Ivy said it, his eyes were drawn downwards. The glove was swinging off his kneecap and he had a perfect – *perfectly gruesome* – view down the open end. There was a hand – a whole hand – a whole *wriggling* hand – still inside.

"Ew!" Ash shuddered.

"I did tell you not to look." Ivy grinned.

The Gory Glove quickly reached Ash's chest. "It's going to strangle me," he cried, his heart thumping as its leathery fingers stretched towards his neck.

"Nonsense," said Ivy. "It just wants you to read the note it's written. Look."

Sure enough, the Gory Glove had stopped climbing and was waving the sheet of yellow paper under Ash's nose.

"Er ... thank you," he said, gingerly taking the edge of the note from the glove's outstretched hand.

The Gory Glove seemed instantly happy. It leapt off Ash's chest and scurried back to the reception desk, where it sat dangling two fingers off the edge of the table, as if it was sitting on a swing.

"So, what does it say?" Ivy peered over Ash's shoulder as they both read the note.

Wellcome!

"Aw! Isn't that lovely?" said Ivy, giving the Gory Glove a big thumbs up.

"Very nice," said Ash weakly. His heart was still racing. "Although there should only be one 'l' in welcome, you know."

"Grrr!" Ivy threw her arms in the air and growled at him in frustration. "Honestly, Ash!" she cried. "A magic spooky glove writes us a note – a really friendly note, as it happens – and all you can do is worry about the spelling. Can't you see how amazing this place is? Are you even going to try and settle in at Grave Grange?"

"I am trying," said Ash, crossly. "I just went to the library! Even though it's just about the most terrifying room I've ever seen. And guess who was in there?"

"Shh!" said Ivy, holding up a finger. "Listen. Can you hear that?"

The glove held up a finger too.

Someone was singing.

"That must be Dad," said Ivy. "See how much he loves it here, Ash, even if you don't. He's singing to himself in the kitchen while he cooks."

"Er... I don't think that's Dad singing," said Ash gently. "It sounds like a woman ... and I think that's ... opera."

Rich, round notes wafted through the air. It definitely didn't sound like one of Dad's favourite Elvis tunes.

"Yikes!" Ash leapt backwards as the

warbling ghost of an enormous woman wearing a shimmering silver dress, and a sort of Viking helmet with horns on it, materialized in front of them.

The phantom opera singer was as big and round as a hot-air balloon and she was floating about a metre off the ground.

"WELCOME TO GRAAAAAAVE GRAAAAAANGE," she sang, kissing Ivy on both cheeks. "Mwah! Mwah!"

Then she floated towards Ash and kissed him too. "Mwah! Mwah!"

"Ahhhh!" Ash shuddered as great gusts of tomb-chilled air whooshed past his ears.

"YOU WILL KNOW WHOOOO I AM, OF COURSEEEEE," she sang in a rich Italian-sounding accent. "I AAAAAM THE WOOOOORLD FAMOUS CONTESSAAAAAA."

Ash and Ivy looked at each other blankly. They had never heard of her. But Ivy gave a little bow.

"Er ... it's an honour to meet you, Contessa," she said. "Do you know our Grandpa Digby, by any chance? Only, we can't find him, and he promised he'd be here."

"OLD DIG GRAAAAAVES?" The Contessa gave a dismissive wave of her transparent hand. "HAVEN'T SEEEEEEN HIM FOR DAAAAAAYS," she replied, still singing. "NOT SINCE HE VOWED HE WOULD VISIT YOOOOOOUUUU LIVING ONES AND MAAAAAKE YOU COMEEEEE TO GRAAAAAVE GRAAAANGE."

"*Make* us come?" said Ash, forcing himself to speak, even though he hated talking to strangers (especially dead, singing ones). "What do you mean, *make* us co—"

But Ivy interrupted him as usual.

"Where's Grandpa Digby now?" she cried. "Are you sure you don't know?"

The Contessa ignored all their questions. "WEEEE AAAARE SOOOO GLAAAAD YOUUUU ARE HEEEERE," she trilled, bursting into song again. "GHOSTS NEEEEEED AN AUDIENCE OR WE FADE, FADE, FADE..." Her booming voice died away to a whisper as if to make the point.

"An audience?" Ash was confused. What did she mean? Was she suggesting Grandpa Digby had "made" them come all the way to Grave Grange just so they could see some sort of performance? Surely they hadn't given up their old home, and moved to a haunted hotel miles from anywhere, simply to hear the Contessa sing opera?

But she spread her arms wide and began to bellow something about "GLORIOUS GHOSTS AAAAND SPOOOOOOKS SUPREME, PHANTOMS FAIR AAAND—"

Just at that moment, Harold the Headless Huntsman burst through the wall behind the reception desk.

"Whoa!" Even Ivy jumped a bit at the sight of him.

Ash slunk back. "And what about you, Harry?" he muttered under his breath. "What are you going to do to entertain us? Juggle?" He couldn't believe he had been brave enough to speak, but the banging in the pipes was louder than ever and the Headless Huntsman had no head (so no ears) to hear him with anyway.

Even so, it made Ash feel better to say something for once, instead of just screaming or hiding under his hat. Grandpa Digby had made promises. But nothing was what it seemed around here. Ash had made a giant effort not to run away from the hotel at first sight. He had tried his best to fit in. But why? What was the point if Grandpa Digby wasn't even going to show up and explain what they were doing here? A feeling of anger was bubbling inside Ash's chest like a boiling kettle.

"WITH NOOOO ONE TO SEEEE US, GHOSTS FLICKER AND FAAAADE," sang the Contessa in deep, sorrowful tones, as she waltzed slowly with the Headless Huntsman around the room.

"Flicker and fade!" echoed the high-pitched voice of a little girl, followed by a rude raspberry-blowing sound, just as a battered brass candlestick flew past Ash's head.

"That's the poltergeist," hissed Ivy, squeezing his arm. "Sorry. I should have told you. I met her before. She's invisible."

"No I'm not! Not if I don't want to be!" The pale shape of little girl in a long white dress, with ribbons in her ringlet hair, swirled round and round above their heads. "The Contessa is right," she bawled. "Ghosts need attention. I NEED ATTENTION!"

"OH DOOOO BE QUIET, MIRABELLE," belted out the Contessa.

"I AM THE STAAAAAR!"

So that was it. Ash suddenly understood.

He looked around at the ghosts who had gathered in the hall: the demon diva, the spoilt poltergeist, the Gory Glove and the Headless Huntsman – not to mention the strange, staring stuffed fish.

"You're showing off," he said slowly. "All of you. That's why we've been dragged here, isn't it? Just so you can have people to show off to ... so you have people to scare."

For a moment, Ash felt triumphant. He was right. He had solved the mystery of why Grandpa Digby had summoned them to Grave Grange. No wonder the old ghost hadn't dared to show his face since. His whole plan to bring the family here so this crazy collection of spooks didn't get bored wafting around the crumbling hotel with nobody new to haunt – just three old ladies who were practically ghosts themselves.

The Contessa leant forward in stunned silence.

The dead fish opened and closed its mouth in surprise.

The Gory Glove raised a finger.

Mirabelle gently replaced the candlestick she was about to throw.

Even the Headless Huntsman seemed to sense something was up and he slunk back against the wall.

"That's better! Now you're listening," said Ash boldly. But he realized almost instantly it wasn't his words which had got their attention at all.

There was another sound – a shrill ringing sound – echoing round the stony hall.

CHAPTER SIXTEEN: *RING!*

Ring!

Ivy couldn't believe her ears.

"That sounds like a telephone," she said in excitement.

There were three reasons why Ivy was surprised by the sound:

One: There was no sign of a telephone anywhere in the hall.

Two: It couldn't be Dad's mobile she could hear ringing – they'd been trying to get reception ever since they'd first driven into Darkmoor, but there wasn't so much as a flicker.

Three: Even if Grave Grange had suddenly got mobile reception, this didn't sound like Dad's Elvis ringtone. This high-pitched ring sounded like a screaming banshee.

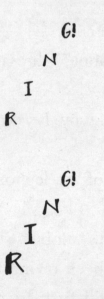

The sound seemed to be getting louder and higher by the second, as if the phone was actually screeching at her to pick it up.

The Grave Grange spooks weren't any help at all. They were all floating about with their mouths wide open. (Those of them who had mouths. Which didn't include Headless Harold or the Glove, of course).

"THE TELEPHONE NEVER RIIIIIINGS!" warbled the Contessa.

"Never, ever!" agreed Mirabelle the poltergeist, excitedly throwing sheets of yellow notepaper in the air.

"But where is it?" said Ivy, panic fluttering inside her. "I need to answer it. It might be guests." If no one new had stayed here for twenty-five years, they couldn't afford to let a single booking escape.

"Guests?" The ghosts laughed, as if this was the funniest thing anybody had ever said. But, in the end, the Gory Glove came to her rescue.

It pointed a finger towards a deep drawer in the bottom of the desk. Sure enough, when Ivy opened it she saw an old-fashioned telephone, vibrating with impatience as it rang and rang.

"Hello?" Ivy picked up the receiver – in fact, she picked up the whole phone. It really was an old fashioned one.

"ISN'T IT MARVELLOUS?" trilled the Contessa. "STAAAATE OF THE AAART TECHNOLOGY."

"Shhh!" said Ivy. "I can't hear if you keep singing like that."

"CHEEEEEEK! TELLING MEEEE, THE WORLD FAMOUS SONGBIRD, TOOOO BEEEE QUIET!" The Contessa was so furious her faint silvery shape actually turned purple with rage (like a giant floating blueberry). But she did (eventually) stop singing.

"Hello?" said Ivy again. "Yes. This is Grave Grange Hotel. Ivy, your receptionist speaking. How may I help you?"

"Who is it?" hissed Ash.

Ivy held up her hand for absolute silence. (It turned out that was a mistake because it meant she was holding the earpiece in the air too.)

"Of course," she said, bringing the telephone back down to her ear. "That's no trouble at all. We'll expect you tomorrow,

Mr Smith. Goodbye."

She hung the earpiece back in its cradle and grinned at Ash and the Grave Grange spooks.

"That was Mr and Mrs Smith," she said. "They want to come and stay at the hotel."

"Guests?" said Ash. Or at least that's what Ivy imagined he probably said. His voice was drowned out by the Contessa opening her mouth as wide as a cave and launching into full-blown opera mode.

"GUESTS. WEEEE'VE GOT GUESTS. TRA LAA LAAAAAAAA!"

And with that, she vanished.

"Hurrah! I love guests," cried Mirabelle. She picked up the candlestick she had so carefully put down a few moments before and threw it at the wall. Then she too disappeared, giggling with delight.

As Ivy looked around the reception hall, she saw that all the spooks had gone – the Headless Huntsman and the Gory Glove too. Even the Staring Salmon had closed its eyes.

"I wonder why they all vanished like that?" she said.

"What do you expect? They're ghosts. And ghosts can't be trusted," said Ash. "Didn't you hear what the Contessa said about Grandpa Digby making us come here? Perhaps he can't be trusted either."

Ivy thought about this for a moment, and then shrugged.

"If Grandpa Digby did make us come, it was only because he knew being the chef at the hotel would be Dad's perfect job," she said. "I'm sure he'll come back soon and explain everything. But until he does, I'm going to do everything I can to welcome our new guests to Grave Grange."

With that, she turned on her heel and went upstairs to choose the best possible room for Mr and Mrs Smith.

CHAPTER SEVENTEEN: POO! WAS THAT YOU?

"Poo! Was that you?" Ash held his nose.

"No it was not!" Ivy looked indignant. They were busy getting a huge dark-red bedroom ready for Mr and Mrs Smith. "I thought it was you!" She giggled, wafting her hand in front of her face. "I thought you'd been eating Dad's Brussels sprout cookies."

Ash laughed. It felt great to be joking around with his twin like this again – just like they used to sometimes back in their old flat.

"Listen, Ives," he said taking a large gulp of (smelly) air. "I know the success of the hotel means so much to you ... and to Dad too. I'm going to try and be a bit braver from now on. I promise."

He really meant it too.

"Thank you!" Ivy's eyes sparkled and she squeezed his arm. "That's brilliant, Ash!"

Then, before things could get too soppy, she threw a big white sheet over her head and made a spooky noise like a ghost.

"WHOOOOOOOOOOOO!"

"Give that here!" Ash grabbed the clean sheet from her and started to put it on the enormous four-poster double bed.

"Ivy?" he whispered, glancing up at the dark-red curtains above him and the dark-red paint on the walls. "Doesn't the colour in this room remind you of—"

"Jam!" said Ivy brightly.

Ash had been thinking of something far more terrible, but he'd only just made his solemn promise to be braver. "Yes. That's it," he agreed in his best "I am VERY brave" voice. "Strawberry jam."

"Wow!" cried Ivy. "You've just given me an amazing idea. Let's call this room the Strawberry Jam Suite. Posh hotels always have fancy names for their rooms."

"Right!" said Ash. "Strawberry Jam Suite it is, then." (Secretly, he couldn't help feeling it sounded more like a sticky pudding than a room. But Ivy seemed so excited, he didn't like to spoil it for her.) It sounded a lot better than BLOOD RED ROOM OF DOOM, which is what he'd been thinking of!

The Strawberry Jam Suite was certainly the fanciest bedroom Grave Grange had to offer. As the Smiths were the first new guests to arrive at the hotel for twenty-five years, it seemed only fair that they should have the finest treatment possible. (Even if the room was still rather smelly).

"We'd better let some air in," said Ash, stumbling towards the window, clutching his nose again. "Where can that dreadful pong be coming from?"

But, as he came round to the other side of the enormous bed, Ash froze.

A huge grey dog was lying on the floor.

Ash did not like dogs.

There were three reasons why:

One: Ash was allergic to dogs. (Dogs made him sneeze.)

Two: Ash was frightened of dogs (especially big dogs, with big sharp teeth).

Three: (Actually. . .) Ash did not like little dogs either. Ash had once been chased all the way home from school by a pug.

But this dog was absolutely enormous –
the size of small pony, with the teeth and
claws of a bear.

The massive dog lifted its humongous head
and stared up at him with huge red eyes.

Ash didn't dare to move.

"Ivy…" he whispered. "There's a grey
hound, lying on the rug."

"A greyhound?" Ivy peered over the edge of the bed.

"No." Ash had researched dogs in the town library at home. (It's always good to know your enemy.) He had seen pictures of greyhounds. Greyhounds are skinny, elegant dogs built for racing, like whippets. This dog wasn't skinny and it definitely wasn't elegant. This dog was built for eating things (probably children).

"Not a greyhound," he said. "A *grey* hound. An absolutely gigantic one." The dog was the colour of bonfire smoke, as grey as the fog on the moors. "Of course!" Ash whispered. "It's a ghost hound. I should have known."

That only made the giant dog even more terrifying.

"Ooh! Isn't she magnificent?" said Ivy, leaning over the bed.

"She?" Ash was still staring into the dog's huge blood-red eyes. He couldn't tear his gaze away. "How do you know it's a she?" he whispered.

"She's got a name tag. It says her name's MISTY – that's usually a girl's name," said Ivy, pointing a finger. "Look."

"Careful!" gasped Ash, leaping backwards. "She'll rip your hand off."

But the dog didn't move.

"I don't think ghosts can bite!" Ivy laughed.

Ash wasn't prepared to put that to the test. All his promises to be brave were forgotten as he slunk back against the window. Ivy was right, though. The dog did have a name tag. It was hanging from a thick leather collar with a ring of sharp steel spikes all around it.

"Good, Misty. Nice, Misty," he said

nervously.

The huge hound leapt to her feet.

"She likes you!" cried Ivy. "She's wagging her tail."

"Likes me?" Ash cowered behind the curtain.

But the ghost hound bounded forward and threw her huge foggy paws around his neck.

"Agh!" cried Ash. "Down, girl. Get off! Sit!" He tried every dog command he'd ever heard. Ivy was no help at all – she was lying on the bed laughing so hard that she had to clutch her tummy.

"It looks like Misty wants to dance with you," she squealed.

Ash was surprised by the strange, snuggly touch of Misty's paws around his neck. This wasn't the chilly feeling he'd got from Grandpa Digby or the ice-cold air of the Contessa. This was like steam – warm steam. He couldn't feel the weight of Misty's paws exactly, but he could sense their shape, pressing down on him with a gentle cosiness. In spite of everything, it made him smile ... just for a moment. And then...

"Yikes! What's that?" he cried, ducking out from under the dog's paws.

Something wet, green and oozy was dripping down his shoulder.

Ivy was laughing so hard now she could barely even speak.

"It's drool!" she spluttered. "Ghost-dog slobber."

"Yuk!" cried Ash. "It's like slime – green, ghostly slime!" But he instantly felt terrible. Poor Misty had slunk away back to her rug, and was lying with her head buried between her paws looking up at him with huge embarrassed eyes.

"Oh dear!" Ash suddenly realized the enormous demon dog wasn't fierce at all. She was just anxious. "She's not a warrior. She's a *worrier,*" he whispered.

Ivy giggled. "Takes one to know one, eh, Ash?"

Ash ignored his sister. But she had a point. He would recognize that look of worry anywhere. He had seen it often enough in his own eyes in the mirror.

"Good girl, Misty. It's all right," he said, tiptoeing closer and wiping the green goo off his shoulder with a spare pillowcase.

But as Ash crouched down beside the giant dog, she suddenly looked guiltier than ever, and Ash clutched his nose, reeling backwards.

"Poo!" cried Ivy. "She farted."

Ash chuckled — then quickly covered his mouth with his hand so the poor dog wouldn't notice they were laughing at her.

"At least we know where that terrible smell was coming from," he whispered, throwing open the window.

"She can't stay here," said Ivy firmly. "Everything has to be perfect for Mr and Mrs Smith. We can't have a smelly old ghost dog lying at the foot of their bed."

"But Misty likes it here," said Ash, surprised to find himself defending a dog. "Maybe this was her owner's room and she's been loyally waiting for their return for hundreds of years."

"Let's see who she belonged to, then," said Ivy. "It usually says on the other side of the dog tag. You look. She likes you."

"Me?" Ash stepped back.

"Yes? What happened to your big promise to be brave?" asked Ivy.

"Fine!" Ash had to admit, he hadn't done very well so far... And Misty really did seem to like him. She was still wagging her huge foggy tail. "Right," he said (bravely). Then he crouched down (cautiously) beside her. "Let's find out a bit about you, old girl."

Again, it was a strange sensation. Ash couldn't actually feel the cold metal of the tag between his fingers, but he sensed the motion of turning it and the disc flipped over.

"*This hound belongs to Sir Harold Graves of Grave Grange, Darkmoor*," he read.

"Headless Harold?" said Ivy.

"Could be," Ash agreed. "I suppose if he's a huntsman, he would have had hounds. Hold on, though... if his real name's Sir Harold Graves, that might mean we're related. He might be our distant ancestor."

"Cool!" Ivy whistled through her teeth. "You see! I bet that's why Grandpa Digby was so keen for us to move. Because we

130

belong here. Grave Grange is our ...
what-do-you-call-it?"

"Ancestral home?" said Ash, as Misty laid
her foggy head on his knee.

"Yeah, that's it. Ancestral home," said Ivy
grandly, sticking her nose in the air. "I might
be Lady Ivy Graves of Grave Grange..."

"Oh no!" Ash buried his head in his
hands. The last thing he needed was Ivy
deciding she was a grand lady of the manor.
But when he looked up again, he saw that
she was biting her lip.

Ash hardly ever saw Ivy look worried.

"I just wish we knew where Grandpa
Digby was," she said. "Then he could
explain everything."

But Ash had spotted something outside
the window.

"Wait! Maybe we're in luck!" He leapt
to his feet. A pale shimmer had caught his

eye. Could that be Grandpa Digby's spirit floating home across the moors at last?

But, for once, it wasn't a ghost Ash saw. He blinked.

It was a car. A huge, white, shiny car.

"The Smiths," he gasped. "They're here early!"

CHAPTER EIGHTEEN: WELCOME TO GRAVE GRANGE

"Welcome to Grave Grange!" said Ivy, grinning so hard her cheeks hurt, as Mr and Mrs Smith made their way across the reception hall towards her. "We do hope you'll have a pleasant stay."

Ivy was determined to make a good impression. Even Ash was trying his best. (He'd taken Misty to his own room and astonishingly let her lie down on his own bed, after they'd hurried her out of the Strawberry Jam Suite at the sight of the

Smiths' approaching car.) Meanwhile, Dad was whipping up a special appetizer for the new arrivals. He really was in his element here at the hotel, clattering around in the kitchen, trying out new recipes from dawn to dusk – all of which seemed to delight the ancient grey ladies. But Ivy knew, if her family were going to remain at Grave Grange, they'd need more than the near-death McEver sisters to keep the business alive. They needed proper guests with money to pay their bills.

Mr and Mrs Smith looked like they had money – quite a lot of money if the big, white, shiny car was anything to go by. And they seemed to have a lot of expensive-looking luggage too. Ash was now staggering under the weight of six matching white suitcases, as he attempted to bring them in over the drawbridge. All Ivy could see of him were his feet poking out from under the enormous mound of bags.

"Apologies. Our porter is very slow," she said, waving her hand dismissively towards Ash. "He's a bit weedy actually, as I'm sure you noticed. We'll be getting a new one soon. A really strong one."

"Right," growled Mr Smith (who looked like a very round, very cross grizzly bear – in a very fancy white suit). "As long he doesn't expect a tip."

"Oh no," said Ivy, grinning more widely than ever. "It's all part of the service here at Grave Grange, Mr Smith."

"I've got all my best frocks in those bags," snapped Mrs Smith (who looked like a very tall, very cross flamingo – with very high-heeled shoes and a very big blonde wig). "That boy better be careful!"

"Careful is Ash's middle name," said Ivy reassuringly. (Actually, Ash's middle name was Kevin, but she'd have said anything to try and please the new guests.) At least the Grave Grange ghosts were keeping out of the way. The last thing she wanted was any strange paranormal activity right now... It was bad enough that the salmon kept glaring at the new arrivals from inside his glass case. (Until that moment, Ivy had never really known the alarming range of menacing expressions a dead fish could manage.)

Luckily, the Smiths didn't seem to be paying any attention to the salmon – or to have even noticed him at all. (Perhaps

that's why the poor fish was so cross.)

Ivy smiled extra hard, just in case. But, the harder she smiled, the more it seemed to her that Mr and Mrs Smith were determined not to smile back.

They glanced around the draughty hall in dismay.

"We were expecting something a bit more modern," said Mr Smith with a grunt. "Have you got a pool?"

"Oh yes," said Ivy. "A lovely outdoor pool. Perhaps if the weather clears up later you could try it." She crossed her fingers behind her back, hoping that the low grey clouds and endless drizzle would deter Mr and Mrs Smith from ever going to investigate the murky black pond behind the kitchen bins. It was the closest thing Grave Grange had to a "pool".

"And, as for Dartmoor, well! We didn't think much of that, did we dear?" said Mrs

Smith dismally.

"Actually," said Ash, staggering into the hall and dropping the suitcases at last. "It's not *Dart*moor, Mrs Smith. It's *Dark*mo—"

"Did you see any ponies?" asked Ivy, cutting Ash off as quickly as she could and shooting him a dagger-sharp stare. "I've heard there are some very cute ones on Dar— on the moor."

"Ponies?" Mr Smith snorted. "We could barely see the road in front of us, there was so much fog."

"Oh dear. That is a shame," said Ivy. "Still, I'm sure you'll enjoy the view from your bedroom window. The Strawberry Jam Suite is our deluxe premier room." (She remembered reading the phrase "deluxe premier room" on one of the fancy hotel websites she used to look at on the internet back home – the sort of place with swirly doors and spa treatments. The sort of place – she couldn't help thinking – that the Smiths would much rather be staying in.)

"If you just give our porter a moment to catch his breath," she said, glancing at Ash, who was still bent double from the effort of heaving all the suitcases in from the car. "Then he'll take you and your luggage up to your room so you can freshen up, before our adventurous chef serves his delicious and daring dinner menu in the dining room." (She'd seen a dinner menu described as "daring" on a website too – privately she thought Dad's flavour combinations weren't just daring... they were downright dangerous. But she kept that thought to herself.)

"Come on then, kid. Jump to it!" said Mr Smith, snapping his fingers so that Ash would pick up the mountain of bags. "Chop, chop!"

It was Ivy's turn to receive a sharp look

from her brother. But, before she could even give him a quick thumbs up of encouragement, all thought of the suitcases was forgotten.

CHAPTER NINETEEN: A GHOSTLY HOWL

A ghostly howl shook the air.

"Misty!" cried Ash, stumbling over the pile of luggage he had dropped at his feet. "I need to go to her." The poor ghost hound sounded distressed. Maybe she was feeling lonely, or frightened, shut up in his room by herself.

"What was that?" screamed Mrs Smith. "It had better not be a dog. I hate dogs. They leave hair everywhere."

"Not this one," said Ash encouragingly.

"Just a little drool. And don't worry if you're allergic, she won't even make you snee—"

Ash froze as his words were drowned out by an even louder sound than Misty's howling.

CHAPTER TWENTY: THINGS MAY SEEEEM STRAAAAANGE WHEN YOU STAAAAY AT GRAAAVE GRAAAAANGE!

"THINGS MAY SEEEEM STRAAAANGE WHEN YOU STAAAAY AT GRAAAVE GRAAAANGE. TRA, LA LAAA. TRA, LAAAA, LAAAAA. TRA LAAA LAAAAAAAAAAAA!"

The reception hall was filled from floor to rafters with the ghostly sound of phantom opera.

"Don't worry, Mr and Mrs Smith," said Ivy brightly. "That's just the Contessa. She's one of our other ... erm, guests. She's been ... erm, *visiting* here for years and years. Very famous, actually."

"I hate opera," grunted Mr Smith. "I hate all singing. I don't see the point in it."

"Right, well, er... I'll ask her to practise a little more quietly," said Ivy, still grinning as widely as she could in an attempt to be welcoming – although she wasn't sure the Smiths deserved to be welcomed. They did seem rather rude. But if Grave Grange had any chance at being a successful hotel, she would have to learn to be polite to anyone who wanted to come and stay.

"As soon as our porter takes your luggage upstairs I'm sure he'll ask the dog to be quiet too!" she said, thrusting the largest of the six white suitcases into Ash's arms, as Misty howled again.

"Hurry up!" she hissed in his ear. "We need to get the Smiths to their room before any of the spooks reappear." From the approaching volume of the Contessa's song, it sounded like she might be about to materialize in the middle of the reception hall at any moment – and if Mr Smith didn't like opera singing, Ivy was pretty certain he'd like long-dead phantom opera singers even less.

"Fine," whispered Ash. "I want to check on Misty anyway."

Ivy bent down, and was about to pick up another suitcase to add to his pile, when the handle shot out of her fingers and the case flew through the air across the room.

"Mirabelle!" cried Ivy, recognizing the

work of the poltergeist at once. "Put that suitcase down, right now."

"Who the dickens is Mirabelle?" roared Mr Smith.

"My bag!" shrieked Mrs Smith, as it shot past her ear.

"My frocks!" she screamed a moment later, as the case hit the floor and burst open, spilling out mounds of white dresses like a silky-looking snowdrift.

"That's it!" said Mr Smith. "Don't bother taking our bags anywhere. We're checking out of this mad hotel."

"Wait," said Ivy, scrambling across the floor on her hands and knees and stuffing Mrs Smith's frocks back into the open case. "It was just the wind that made your luggage fly across the room like that."

"Wind?" said Mr Smith.

Ivy knew it was a pretty feeble excuse – especially as a Mr Smith's spectacles had just flown off the end of his nose and were now whizzing round the room too. From the way they were darting about, Ivy guessed that Mirabelle was probably wearing them on her own (invisible) nose.

Luckily, without his specs, Mr Smith didn't seem to notice the fleeting figure of Harold the Headless Huntsman passing through the reception hall just a metre or two in front of his face. And Mrs Smith was too busy stamping her feet and screaming about her dresses to see anything at all.

They didn't even notice the Gory Glove, which had scuttled up on to the reception desk and was waving a piece of yellow paper in the air. Ivy saw the words HOTELL BILLE scrawled across it in green ink.

She leapt to her feet and swiftly swept the Gory Glove into a drawer with one hand, whilst grabbing the floating spectacles from mid-air with the other.

"Appetizer, anybody?" said Dad, choosing this moment to appear from the kitchen, brandishing a tray of the special bite-sized treats he'd prepared for the guests.

"Oh yes, do have something to eat," said Ivy, handing Mr Smith back his specs. She instantly wished she hadn't.

Mr Smith peered down at the tray of nibbles in disgust. "Are those eyeballs?" he gasped

"Pickled eggs in fruit jelly." Dad grinned. "Try one. They're delicious."

"Absolutely scrumptious!" agreed (probably) Enid, appearing in the doorway behind him.

"Delectable," echoed (probably) Ethel.

"I've had three. They have made me a bit gassy, though," grinned (probably) Edna.

"Arghhh!" screamed Mrs Smith. "Ghosts!"

"No," said Ivy quickly. "They're not ghosts."

"They're the only ones who aren't," muttered Ash.

"These are the McEver sisters," said Ivy.

"And I'm pleased to say they are very much alive."

"They look old," said Mrs Smith rudely. "I hate old people." She frowned and touched her own powdery-pink cheek as if she was afraid that wrinkles might be catching.

If the old ladies were offended, they didn't show it.

They smiled cheerily at the new guests . . . although (probably) Edna did burp very loudly.

"Sorry! I told you those pickles were gassy," she said with a giggle.

But Mr and Mrs Smith were already striding across the room.

"We don't want to meet your freaky guests," said Mr Smith, jabbing a furious finger at Ivy. "We don't want to eat your revolting food. We don't want to stay another minute at your creepy hotel. We just want to go home."

He turned and headed towards the door, clicking his fingers at Ash without even looking back. "Hurry up and bring those bags!"

"No," said Ash, more loudly than Ivy would ever have thought he'd have dared.

"Pardon?" Mr Smith spun round and glared at him. "What did you say to me?"

"I said no!" Ash's chin was trembling as he spoke. "You can carry your bags yourself if you want to leave."

Ivy had never seen him stand up to anyone before. Now here he was with his cap pushed back off his forehead and his chin in the air.

"Well done, you tell 'em!" cheered one of the three old McEver sisters and the other two clapped their hands.

Dad was opening and closing his

mouth, looking just as amazed as Ivy. "Ash?" he spluttered, as Mr Smith barged past him.

The furious guest reminded Ivy of a big school bully striding across a playground. "Pick up those suitcases!" he bellowed, wagging his finger right under Ash's nose. "Pick them up this instant."

But Ash stood his ground.

"No," he said, and for a moment his small shaky voice was almost a roar (a proper roar − like a mighty Ash-shaped lion). "You've been horrid since the moment you arrived here. We don't want horrid guests at our hotel. It's our home. "

"Home?" Ivy couldn't stop herself gasping in surprise. "Ash? So you do like it here after all?"

"Of course I do. Or at least I'm trying to," said Ash, his roar dying to more of a mumble now. "I just don't want guests who are going to be horrid, that's all."

"Ha!" Mrs Smith snorted. "You really are a silly boy," she said. "All guests are horrid. What does it matter? We're paying you money. That's what running a hotel is all about."

"No," said Ash, so quietly that Ivy wondered if she was the only one who heard him. "It doesn't have to be like that."

Ivy wanted to throw her arms around Ash's neck and cheer him for his courage. She knew he was right. The Smiths *were* terrible people.

But it wasn't as simple as that.

Mrs Smith was right too: they were guests and Grave Grange needed guests – any guests – or they'd have to close down.

"Please," she begged, turning to smile

at Mr and Mrs Smith and not even daring to look Ash in the eye. "*Please*, give us a second chance. Everyone's been a bit cross and things have been a little ... well, a little *strange* ... but we can all start again." She felt a last wild, impossible wave of hope.

She'd be so distracted by Ash, she had barely noticed, but the ghosts had gone quiet at last.

The Contessa had finally stopped singing.

Misty had stopped howling.

The Gory Glove was locked in the drawer.

If Mirabelle was still here being invisible, at least nothing was actually flying round the room.

The Headless Huntsman had disappeared – off hunting somewhere perhaps.

That only left the spooky salmon, and nobody ever paid any attention to him.

With the ghosts out of the way, Ivy felt they really might be able to make a fresh start and convince the Smiths that Grave Grange really was a lovely place to stay.

"You see, you're our very first guests," she explained truthfully. "We'll get better, I promise."

Ash nodded reluctantly.

"Exactly. This is all new for us," assured Dad (who never even seemed to notice the ghosts. He was far too busy in the kitchen). "Whatever the matter is here, I'm sure it's just a few teething problems."

"Teething problems – more like full-blown tooth decay!" said Mrs Smith. "We'll be leaving our online feedback about this place at **STAY-WELL-AWAY.COM**. And it won't be a good review."

"Oh no! Don't do that," cried Ivy. **STAY-WELL-AWAY.COM** was one of the most popular travel sites on the Internet. "Please just give us a chance," she begged. But, as she spoke, the thumping in the wall started again with a great BOOM!

"Yikes!" screamed Mrs Smith, leaping with fright, and almost tripping over the suitcases behind her. "What was that? Giant rats?"

"It's just the pipes," said Ivy quickly. "Don't worry. We're going to get those sorted too."

"Pipes?" said Mr Smith. "Whatever's making that infernal din, it's not the pipes."

"And he's a plumber," said Mrs Smith. "So he should know. You can look him up on **PERFECT-PLUMBERS.COM**. 'No blockage too big!' He's had a hundred per cent satisfaction."

With that, the couple picked up their own suitcases at last and strode out over the drawbridge.

"Oh dear," said Dad, staring down at the

tray of pickles. "Was that my fault? Was it my appetizers, do you think?"

"No, Dad." Ivy gently squeezed his arm. "As you said, some people just aren't ready for 'experimental'."

"I'm sorry," said Ash. "I shouldn't have been so rude to them."

"Nonsense!" said (probably) Edna. Her sisters tutted in agreement.

"They deserved it," said Ivy. "I just wish they could have given Grave Grange a chance."

She looked out over the drawbridge. The Smiths were already climbing back into their shiny white car.

"There's something creepy and unnatural about this place," shouted Mrs Smith. "It doesn't even have a sauna." Then they sped away across the windswept moors.

CHAPTER TWENTY-ONE: HAUNTINGLY AWFUL!

Hauntingly Awful – Minus Five Stars.

Grave Grange Hotel, Darkmoor, should be closed down immediately. Do not stay there ever!

Mr and Mrs Smith

USEFUL 👍

"Oh dear," groaned Ash, as he read on through the appalling review that the Smiths had posted online. "Ivy is not going to like this. She's not going to like it one little bit."

He was standing on his tiptoes in the darkest corner of the darkest attic in the highest tower at Grave Grange. Less than a fortnight ago, Ash wouldn't even have stood alone in a half-lit broom cupboard – let alone a pitch-black cobwebbed attic with bats hanging from the rafters. But he had promised Ivy he would try and find a Wi-Fi connection somewhere at Grave Grange, so they could discover exactly what the Smiths had posted in their review of the hotel.

"I wish I hadn't bothered," he said, as Misty laid her foggy head against his knee. It was the ghost hound who had made him brave enough to come up here to the tower in the first place. With the dog beside him in the dark, Ash realized that he wasn't even reciting his seventeen times table to stay calm.

It had been a whole week now since the day the Smiths had tried to check-in and he had found Misty in the Strawberry Jam Suite. Ash had thought she might want to go back there, now the room wasn't needed again. But Misty had spent every night since curled up on the floor at the end of Ash's bed. (She had even tried to sleep *on* his bed for the first night, but they both soon realized there wasn't enough room for a boy and a horse-sized dog in one small bed – especially as Misty kept stealing the covers and Ash had woken up to find his cheek lying in a truly terrifying pool of drool). With that (and the occasional fart) Misty was banished to the floor, where Ash had made her a soft bed of her own out of an enormous pair of old velvet curtains.

Now Misty followed Ash everywhere. The only time she fled from his heel was if they happened to catch sight of Harold the Headless Huntsman wafting through a wall. For some reason, Misty didn't seem to want to come face-to-face (or face-to-neck) with her old master. *Who could blame her?* Ash thought (the headless huntsman really was *not* a pretty sight). Whatever the reason, Ash was surprised – and delighted – to have such a loyal companion by his side, to help him hold his nerve in the dark and spooky corners of the hotel.

"Oh dear, Misty. Listen to this," he said, reading from the brightly lit screen of the laptop. He read out the three main reasons why the Smiths would not recommend Grave Grange Hotel. Ever.

One: We are not so foolish as to believe in ghosts, but if we were, we would say this place is haunted.

Two: We are not so foolish as to believe in paranormal activity, but if we were, we would say this place is possessed.

Three: We are not so foolish as to have actually tried the food, but the sight and smell of Chef Grave's eyeball appetizers will haunt us for ever.

Ash scanned the rest of the page. "They talk about you, Misty," he said. "Listen: 'Strange howling, echoing across the desolate moors.'"

"Woof!" Misty wagged her tail proudly, as if she actually understood what he was saying (it was probably just because Ash was tickling her foggy belly as he read).

"They also complain about their suitcases flying through the air," he said. "And they

162

say there were sounds 'like a strangled cat'."
Ash giggled. "I think they must mean the
Contessa's singing, don't you?"

Suddenly, Misty pricked her shadowy ears
and turned towards the dark hatch leading
up to the attic.

"Who's there?" said Ash, his heart
pounding as the rungs of the rickety ladder
creaked.

"Only me!" said a familiar voice and
Ivy's head popped up over the top of the
hatch. It was soon followed by the rest of
her body, of course, because (unlike Harold
the Huntsman) Ivy's head was still firmly
attached.

"Oh, it's you," said Ash, but his heart
carried on pounding. He knew how much
the success of the hotel meant to Ivy and
he was terrified of admitting how truly
terrible the Smiths' review of Grave Grange

really was.

"Tell me the worst," she said, her anxious face given a sickly glow by the shining light of the computer screen. "How bad is it? Terrible? Really terrible? Or beyond terrible?"

"It's minus five stars," blurted out Ash quickly, feeling sure that bad news was better told at top speed. He passed her the laptop.

Ivy read in silence for a moment and then sighed a deep, slow, sad sigh.

"It's deadly," she said. "This review is so bad, nobody will ever come and stay at Grave Grange ever again. **STAY-WELL-AWAY.COM** is a really popular website. A hundred and seventy-seven people have seen the review already."

"A hundred and seventy-nine, actually," said Ash, leaning over her shoulder and seeing that the count had already risen. "But it's only a hundred and seventy-eight, if you don't include us." He smiled weakly.

Ivy buried her head in her hands.

"As soon as people see this, they'll stay away for sure. It's all over," she said. "We'll never make a success of this business now, not without new guests to pay the bills. Dad practically cleaned the last pennies out of his bank account to buy the ingredients for the appetizers. There's nothing left. We'll just have to pack up and go home."

"You mean we're giving up?" whispered Ash. He was surprised by how hollow and miserable the thought of leaving this spooky old place made him feel.

But Ivy shook her head, rolled up her sleeves and leapt to her feet – a new determination glowing in her eyes.

"Certainly not!" she said. "We're not giving up. Not yet. But we're going to have to make some changes, that's for sure." Ash leapt to his feet too (which was a mistake, because he hit his head on the beam above him).

"Ouch!" he cried, hopping from foot to foot. "What sort of changes?"

But Ivy had already disappeared down the ladder.

CHAPTER TWENTY-TWO: IF ONLY GRANDPA DIGBY WAS HERE

"If only Grandpa Digby was here," muttered Ivy as she stormed across the reception hall. But Ash had been right all along. The old ghost couldn't be trusted. He had raised their hopes and that wasn't fair. Not now that Dad believed he really could be a hotel chef. Not now that she had fallen head-over-heels in love with Grange Grange too. Ivy adored living at the spooky hotel, where there was never a dull moment and she couldn't bear the thought of returning to their boring old life ever again. Even Ash was coming round to the place. She watched him smile shyly as he whistled for Misty and the spook dog came bounding to his heels.

"If Grandpa Digby's not coming, then it's up to us," she said, calling over her shoulder to him. "We'll have to be the ones to take action!"

"Pardon?" said Ash, putting his hand to his ear.

Ivy wasn't surprised he couldn't hear her. The banging in the pipes had grown louder than ever.

BOOM! BOOM! BOOM!

"Just listen to this place." Ivy groaned. "The Smiths were right. It deserves minus five stars. It's falling down around us." She loved Grave Grange just the way it was, but she knew they were going to have to make big changes to survive.

"Take the library," she said, waving her hand towards the door. "Half the books in there are so old they're written in Ancient Egyptian hieroglyphs, for goodness' sake. There's probably a haunted mummy's tomb in the wall behind the bookcase somewhere."

"The library. . ." said Ash, but Ivy carried on.

"As for the ballroom. . ." She spun around and pointed to the room next door. "It's so old and dusty in there I don't think anyone's actually danced since Harold the Headless Huntsman's tenth birthday party!"

"The library," said Ash again. "And ballroom ... right beside it. I think you might be on to something, Ivy."

But she ignored him (as usual). Whatever

he was muttering about, he seemed to have missed the point – and she was finding it hard enough to concentrate herself with all that banging in the pipes.

"Guests don't like cobwebs and creaky doors," she hollered in Ash's ear. "Guests like hotels with swirly doors ... and saunas ... and spas. The sort of places you see on the Internet. The sort of places which get five shiny stars for every review on **STAY-WELL-AWAY.COM**. That's the sort of place we've got to turn Grave Grange into."

BOOM! BOOM! BOOM! The walls sounded like they were going to crack in half, the thumping sound was so loud.

"First things first," yelled Ivy. "We have to get those pipes mended."

"But it's not the pipes," Ash hollered back. "Mr Smith said so." There was a pause in the banging and Ash spoke quickly. "He may be a mean person, Ivy, and a horrible guest, who writes dreadful reviews, but he is a good plumber. I looked him up on **PERFECT-PLUMBERS.COM**. He really has had a hundred per cent satisfaction."

The banging started again. *Boom! Boom! Boom!*

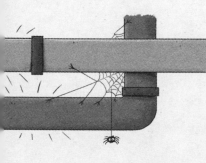

"If Mr Smith says it is not the pipes," shouted Ash. "Then it's not the pipes."

"So what *is* making that awful noise, then, clever-clogs?" said Ivy, shaking her head.

But Ash didn't seem to be listening. *He* was ignoring *her*!

"Shhh!" He threw himself flat on the floor (which Misty seemed to think was some sort of hilarious game for spooky dogs;

she was trying to ghost-lick his face with her shadowy tongue.)

"Sit!" said Ash firmly. Then he pressed his ear against the rumbling wall.

"You're asking the wrong question, Ivy," he said in his most irritating pay-attention-to-the-details voice. "It's not *what* is making this noise. It's *who*?"

CHAPTER TWENTY-THREE: KNOCK, KNOCK! WHO'S THERE?

Knock, Knock!

"Who's there?" Ash took off his beloved baseball cap and pressed his head flat against the thick wall of the reception hall. He rapped his knuckles hard against the cold stone. "Knock twice if you can hear me."

Knock! Knock!

A clear reply came back.

"Ivy, fetch a glass," said Ash. He

173

remembered reading somewhere that if you press an empty glass against a wall you can hear through to the other side.

But, before Ivy could move, the Gory Glove had taken it upon itself to up-end the ink well from the reception desk, splashing green ink all over the floor.

"Er ... thank you," said Ash, taking the mucky pot from the Gory Glove's fingers.

"Hello? Can you hear me?" he said, pressing the pot closer to the wall. "Is that you in there?"

"Who?" said Ivy, crouching beside him.

"Grandpa Digby, of course!" said Ash. He'd realized the minute Ivy had started going on about the dusty old books in the library and the old ballroom right next door. "Don't you remember? He told us how he'd once got stuck in the walls here for six whole weeks. I can't believe it's taken us so long. The same thing must have happened on the night of the storm. He must have got wedged inside the wall when he was trying to get back into the reception hall."

Sure enough, they heard a loud groan and a wheezing sound.

"Ash, you found him! You found Grandpa Digby," cheered Ivy. "You really are a hero."

"Excuse me," bellowed the old ghost's spooky voice from deep inside the wall. "Aren't you going to get me out of here, then?"

"That's easy!" said Ash, surprised at his own confidence. He had already thought about this. He'd noticed how the ink which the Gory Glove had splashed on the ground was trickling away through a tiny crack between the base of the wall and the floor.

"Grandpa Digby?" he said boldly. "Remember how you said you were an excellent *slider*? Well, I think I may have found you a teeny-tiny gap. . ."

Ash began to tap on the wall again.

"Follow this sound, Grandpa Digby," he said. "And we'll have you out of there in no time."

Grandpa Digby said three things as he squeezed through the tiny crack.

One: ★★★★★★★!

Two: !!!!!!!

Three (And worst of all): @@@@@@@!

But all of them are far too rude to print.

Yet, in five minutes flat, (very flat − it really was a tight squeeze) Grandpa Digby had slid through the gap and was floating beside them in the hall.

"Hello," said Ash shyly.

"Grandpa Digby!" Ivy cheered.

Misty raised her foggy hackles and barked at the old ghost in surprise.

"Amazing! Well done for getting me out of there, lad!" said Grandpa Digby, patting Ash on the head.

"Brrr!" Ash shivered. He still hadn't put his cap back on, and he leapt backwards as he felt a ghostly chill, like a jolt of freezing electricity, run through him.

He wondered if he would *ever* quite get used to being around ghosts.

"Whoops!" said Grandpa Digby. "Sorry about that. Being dead plays havoc with your circulation." He blew on his fingers as if trying to warm them up.

"Don't worry. It's just nice to have you back," said Ash — and he really meant it. Things were going to be so much easier now Grandpa Digby was here to help.

But he was surprised to see the old ghost frowning at him as he reached down to pick up his cap and pull it back on.

"Don't bother with that old thing. I like your new look much better," said Grandpa Digby. "I can see your face."

Ash glanced up.

"Whoa!" He caught sight of himself in the old cracked mirror above the reception desk. His hair was sticking up in crazy spikes and it had a bright green streak right down the middle, where the ink had come off his fingers.

"Very edgy! It suits you," chuckled Grandpa Digby.

"Yes!" Ash grinned. Then he tossed his cap away as if he was Miriam, throwing an unwanted candlestick across the room. Misty bounded after it. "I like my new style too!" he said.

It certainly made him *look* much braver, even if he didn't feel (totally) brave inside. Not quite yet.

CHAPTER TWENTY-FOUR: THE CLOCK STRUCK TWELVE

The clock struck twelve — BONG!

"Midnight," said Ivy. But she wasn't tired. She was excited. They had agreed to meet Grandpa Digby in the library. Now he was back, everything was going to be all right. He would know what to do about the Smiths' terrible review on **STAY-WELL-AWAY.COM**. He would help them save Grave Grange. After all, it had been Grandpa Digby's idea to persuade Dad to come and work here in the first place.

"Ah, there you are, young nippers," he said, sliding out from a gap behind the grandfather clock.

(*Perhaps that was why they were called grandfather clocks*, Ivy thought. *Because grandfathers could hide behind them.*)

"Agh!" said Ash, leaping with surprise. Ivy giggled. Poor Ash never could seem to get used to the shock of ghosts appearing out of thin air. She hadn't even flinched.

"Apologies for the late hour," said Grandpa Digby, as Ivy and Ash sat down in a pair of huge leather armchairs. "I thought it might be best to meet after your dad and the old Grey Ladies had gone to bed. It's sometimes best if we ghosts don't show ourselves."

"But that's what I don't understand," said Ivy. "You've shown yourself to us. The others have too. The Contessa. Headless Harold, the Gory Glove ... all of them."

She pointed to Misty who, loyal as ever, had followed Ash into the library and was lying in a huge, foggy heap at his feet.

"That's because we've made an exception for you two nippers. I told my spooky pals we needed your help," said Grandpa Digby.

"Funny way of showing it," muttered Ash.

But Ivy was still confused.

"That doesn't make sense," she said. "The ghosts appeared when the Smiths arrived too. Mirabelle started throwing things. The Contessa was singing. There was pretty much spooky mayhem."

"Mayhem?" Grandpa Digby chuckled mischievously. "Sounds marvellous."

"No!" said Ivy, surprising herself at how cross she sounded. "It wasn't marvellous. It's ruined everything." She was usually the first one to love a bit of mayhem and madness – but not now. Not if it meant they would have to close the hotel. "The Smiths have written a terrible review," she explained. "And—"

Grandpa Digby held up a foggy hand.

"Tell me," he said. "Did these silly Smith people actually *see* any of my ghostly friends?"

"Well, no..." Ivy thought about it. "I suppose not. Mirabelle was invisible when she was throwing things. And the Contessa was singing through the walls. There was the Salmon..."

"Nobody ever pays any attention to him, poor old fish," said Grandpa Digby.

Ivy nodded. "Harold the Headless Huntsman appeared – but only briefly. The Smiths might have caught a glimpse, but nothing more than that."

"Excellent!" Grandpa Digby chortled

with delight. "A wee glimpse does so add to the fun."

"Fun?" cried Ivy. Why wasn't Grandpa Digby taking this seriously? "The Grave Grange ghosts might as well have sat on our guests' knees in broad daylight and pinched their noses," she said. "It may only have been a glimpse or two, but the Smiths still guessed that the hotel is haunted."

"Although in their review they said they weren't silly enough to believe in ghosts," added Ash.

"Pah! Even better! Dunderheaded doubters!" said Grandpa Digby. "Your silly stuck-up Smith guests saw just enough to make them *wonder*. Things moved in a strange way. They heard peculiar sounds. Shivers ran down their spines. There was mystery and eeriness." He chuckled. "We ghosts live for mystery and eeriness ...

well, maybe not *live* exactly, but you get the point."

"Is that what the Contessa was singing about?" asked Ash. "When she said that ghosts need an audience or they flicker and fade."

Ivy remembered how cross Ash had been when he'd heard that. He'd accused the ghosts of showing off. And he had been right.

"Without anyone to believe in us ... or to *wonder* at least ... ghosts are nothing but pale spirits who vanish like steam," said Grandpa Digby, melting away behind the clock again as if to prove his point.

"Wait!" said Ivy. "Come back." She stormed up to the clock and shouted through the crack. "Are you saying that you persuaded us to come to the hotel just so you and the other ghosts could scare

184

the guests?" She felt as if Grandpa Digby had tricked them — their move here been nothing but a spooky joke. "You turned our whole lives upside down, all so that the Grave Grange ghosts can haunt people!"

"No . . . not entirely." Grandpa Digby slid out from behind the clock looking sheepish. "There are three main reasons why I invited you to come and live at our hotel. . ."

These are the three reasons Grandpa Digby gave:

One: Grandpa Digby had never had the chance to get to know his grandchildren before he died (on the very same day that they were born). Bringing them to the hotel offered the perfect chance to get to know them now.

Two: Grandpa Digby knew that his son (Ivy and Ash's dad) had always longed for the opportunity to be a chef with his own restaurant. Where better to be a chef than in a large hotel?

Three: (Just as the twins had guessed) Grave Grange was their ancestral home. There had been members of the Graves family living at Grave Grange ever since the time of their distant relative (the now headless) Sir Harold Graves nearly four hundred years ago.

Grandpa Digby, hadn't lived here himself while he was alive, of course. He had lived in a flat above a chip shop ... but, restless in his grave, his spirit had been drawn to Grave Grange and he had been haunting it ever since. Now he wanted his son and grandchildren to have the chance to enjoy it while they were still actually alive.

"Oh dear!" said Ivy. Those were wonderful reasons. She couldn't deny it. She was desperate to get to know Grandpa Digby better. She longed for Dad to be happy, living his dream as a chef. And she was especially excited to learn that she was a Graves of Grave Grange ... their grand "ancestral" home.

"But it's just not going to work." She sighed. "You want us to bring guests here so that you can haunt them. But if you haunt our guests they'll run away screaming in terror and won't ever come back – then they'll write dreadful reviews like the Smiths did and we won't earn any money and we'll have to close down the hotel."

"Nonsense. I don't think it's as bad as all that!" said Grandpa Digby.

But Ivy knew she was right.

"Either our family will have to leave Grave Grange, or the ghosts will have to go," she said firmly.

CHAPTER TWENTY-FIVE: GARLIC?

"Garlic?" Ash was confused. "What do you want garlic for, Ivy? It's the middle of the night."

They had just left Grandpa Digby in the library, and both the old spook and Ivy had been in very bad moods by the time the meeting was over.

Now Ivy was turning Dad's kitchen cupboards inside out in a desperate search for garlic.

"How about this?" said Ash, trying to be helpful and holding up an onion instead. "Will this do?"

"No, it will not!" Ivy snapped.

"Whoa! Sorry." Ash stepped back, almost putting his foot right through Misty, who was close by his heels as always. "There's some, if it's so important," he said, pointing to a string of garlic he had just spotted hanging from the pantry door. "What do you want it for, anyway? You're not going to get all experimental and start baking garlic cupcakes or something, are you? We've got enough of that with Dad." Ash wrinkled his nose and laughed, trying to lighten the tone.

But Ivy wasn't laughing.

She grabbed the string of garlic and stormed out of the kitchen door.

"Come on, we'd better follow," said Ash, calling softly to Misty.

He had a horrible feeling that they were heading towards trouble... BIG trouble.

CHAPTER TWENTY-SIX: BAD DOG! SHOO!

"Bad dog! Shoo!" Ivy came to a stop in the middle of the reception hall and spun around to face Ash. She waved the string of garlic at Misty who was still trotting by his heels. The dog seemed to follow Ash everywhere now.

"Go away!" she said again. "Go away! Bad dog! Shoo!" She shook the garlic under the spooky hound's long, drooling nose.

Misty's shadowy tail instantly drooped

between her legs and her big worried eyes stared up at Ivy in surprise.

"Stop it!" Ash gasped, leaping between the two of them. "Leave Misty alone. What's she ever done to you?"

"Driven everyone away from here with her eerie howling, that's what," said Ivy. "You heard Grandpa Digby. He said the Grave Grange ghosts just want to cause trouble and haunt our guests."

"That's not exactly what he said," answered Ash carefully.

But Ivy knew she had to stay firm. "If our family is going to have any chance of making a success of this hotel then Misty will have to leave," she said. "All the ghosts will have to go! Every single spook who is haunting Grave Grange."

"Wait! I'm sure we can all work something

out," said Ash, holding up his arms to protect Misty.

But Ivy shook the string of garlic again. She was fairly certain that waving garlic was what you were supposed to do to get rid of ghosts.

"That means you too," she said, breaking off a whole bulb of the stinky stuff and putting it on top of the spooky salmon's glass case.

"And you!" She waved the string furiously at the Gory Glove, who was perched on the edge of the reception desk swinging its fingers. "You'll all have to go. Every single ghost at Grave Grange. You'll just have to find somewhere new to haunt."

"But..." Ash seemed momentarily lost

for words. He crouched down beside the cowering ghost hound and stroked Misty's shadowy ears. "We can't do that, Ivy."

"We have to." Ivy felt her lip wobble. She didn't want to be mean. She certainly didn't want to upset pale, gentle Misty ... or even the cold, dead fish and the Gory Glove. But she had no choice. "Listen," she said. "Can you hear that?"

"Yes," said Ash. "It's singing... It sounds like it's coming from the kitchen."

"Exactly!" said Ivy. "It's *Dad* singing. He must have gone down there since we got the garlic. He's cooking even though it's the middle of the night."

There was no mistaking it this time. It definitely wasn't the Contessa. The Contessa did not sing Elvis songs. Dad was bellowing the words to the famous Elvis hit "You ain't nothing but a hound dog!"(An unfortunate choice, Ivy thought, considering she had just asked Ash's ghostly hound dog to leave home and never come back.)

"Misty's just a ghost," she said gently. "She's not even alive, Ash. Not any more. But Dad's alive ... more alive than he has been for years. Listen to him. He's happy."

They heard the clatter of pots and pans over his singing.

"Dad loves it here," said Ivy. "He loves being a chef. But he's going to need guests to cook for. Guests who pay money so he can afford to buy ingredients for all his crazy new recipes."

"What about the Grey Ladies?" said Ash. "They're not ghosts. We can't just get rid of them."

"Exactly," said Ivy. "But they don't pay any money either. If we can get proper guests to come to the hotel, we can keep it open. If not, the Grey Ladies will lose their home and so will we."

She swung the string of garlic above her head.

"Go on," she said, "all of you. Shoo!"

She tried desperately not to catch Ash's eye, or listen to the little whimper coming from the enormous spook dog at his heels.

A fat bulb of garlic flew off the string as she lassoed it above her head. It spun in the air ... and passed right through the ghostly figure of Grandpa Digby, who had just slithered under a gap in the dining room door.

"I see you're trying to get rid of us," he said, calmly. "There's just one thing I think you should know..."

"What is it?" said Ivy.

She was too ashamed to even raise her eyes and look at the old spook.

"Garlic gets rid of vampires," he said softly. "Not ghosts. Ghosts come and go as we please. I told you that before, remember?"

"Well you're going to have to go now. I'm sorry," Ivy whispered. "I wish there was another way. I wish we could all stay at Grave Grange together."

But when she raised her eyes, Grandpa Digby had already vanished.

CHAPTER TWENTY-SEVEN: IT WAS (TOO) QUIET

It was quiet.

Too quiet.

Ash sat bolt upright in bed and listened.

Nothing.

Not a squeaking floor board. Not a banging pipe. Not a note of opera. Not the smash of flying china hitting the floor.

Nothing.

"Misty!" he gasped, scrambling to the end of his bed. But he already knew what he would see.

Nothing.

The hound's velvet bed was empty. Misty was gone. And so was every other ghost in Grave Grange.

Ash knew this for certain. He could feel it in his bones.

CHAPTER TWENTY-EIGHT: RING! RING!

Ring! Ring!

Ivy leapt up to answer the telephone.

"Hello?" she said. "Grandpa Digby? Is that you?"

She was vainly hoping it might be the old ghost calling to tell her where he was. It had been three nights since the Grave Grange spooks had all vanished, and she still had no idea where to.

"Pardon?" said a woman's voice on the end of the line. "Grandpa who?"

"Sorry," said Ivy, half-heartedly trying to concentrate on her job. "You've reached Grave Grange Hotel. How can I help you?"

It was silly to think it might have been Grandpa Digby calling. Ivy wasn't even sure ghosts could use the telephone. The Gory Glove had left them a note, at least — and that was probably all she and Ash would ever get.

Gonne Hunting
The hotle is your's now.
Do not worrie about uss.
Writton On behalve of Granddpa
Dug and the ghoosts ov Grave Grange

Gone hunting? What did that even mean? It was all they had written. Then the whole ghostly gang had vanished.

All but the spooky salmon, who was still staring at Ivy from his glass case.

Ivy suspected the other ghosts might have forgotten all about him – poor thing. Or perhaps he had refused to leave. He did have a stubborn glint in his fishy eye. She wondered how Grandpa Digby had persuaded the others to go. Had they all just wafted away in a sulk? Or had Grandpa Digby coaxed them into going – telling them it was their duty to move out of the hotel so that Ivy and her family could make the business work, live here and be happy? Except Ivy wasn't happy – not without Grandpa Digby.

She hadn't even had time to get to know him properly yet. It was all her fault. She had driven him away.

"Hello?" The woman on the telephone raised her voice. "Hello? Are you still there? I'd like to make a reservation, please."

"A reservation?" Ivy snapped out of her daze. "Certainly," she said. "We would be delighted to welcome you to Grave Grange."

This was what she had been waiting for. A second chance. At least Grandpa Digby hadn't vanished in vain. New guests were coming to stay. And this time there wouldn't be any ghosts or ghouls to scare them off.

CHAPTER TWENTY-NINE: GRAVE GRANGE IS *NOT* HAUNTED

"Grave Grange is *not* haunted. Grave Grange is a guaranteed ghost-free hotel," said Ash, repeating the words Ivy had made him practise all day long. Then he smiled (which he had nearly forgotten to do, even though Ivy had made him practise that too). Ivy had also made him wear a home-made name badge she had designed:

MY NAME IS ASH.
HAPPY TO HELP!

"Hello!" The new arrivals, Mr and Mrs Jones, smiled back at him.

They seemed nice. Mr Jones had a big bushy beard like a bird's nest and Mrs Jones had long dangly earrings, which jingled when she moved.

All the same, Ash hated greeting strangers (even nice ones). He wished he hadn't left his cap upstairs, now he'd taken to his new hairstyle. His palms were sweating. He hurriedly wiped them on the back of his trousers, before stretching out his hand and offering to take their suitcase.

"Don't worry. We can manage," said Mr Jones kindly. "It's only the one and it's on wheels anyway."

Mrs Jones was standing at the foot of the drawbridge, staring up at the towering rooftops of Grave Grange.

"Isn't it old!" she said. "And you're absolutely sure it's not haunted, pet?"

"Absolutely sure," Ash reassured her. "There are no ghosts at Grave Grange." He  felt himself blush as he suddenly remembered the Spooky Salmon was still in its glass case on the mantelpiece in the hall. He wondered if he ought to mention it as a point of honesty.

He decided not to.

There were three reasons Ash decided

not to mention the possessed fish:

One: Guests do not like ghosts (not even stuffed, fishy ones).

Two: Nobody ever seemed to notice the Spooky Salmon anyway.

Three: (and this was the strongest reason of all): If he did mention the ghostly fish, Ivy would probably kill him. (If she did kill him, he too might became a ghost ... meaning that Grandpa Digby would have taken the spooks into hiding for no reason ... and Grave Grange could no longer guarantee itself ghost-free.)

"I'm surprised to hear you say there are no spooks here, pet." Mrs Jones was shaking her head. Ash had obviously not done a very good job of reassuring her, in spite of practising Ivy's ghost-free greeting and wearing his NO GHOSTS badge. "Only we thought there would be something because of—"

But before she could finish her sentence they heard the sound of crunching gravel behind them.

Ash spun round.

"Yikes!" His heart began to pound.

But it wasn't ghosts they had heard approaching.

It was guests.

Six more strangers had just arrived in a minibus ... and it was Ash's job to greet them.

"Welcome to Grave Grange. Grave Grange is not haunted. Grave Grange is a guaranteed ghost-free hotel," he mumbled. Then he remembered (yet again) he had forgotten to smile.

"Ghost-free? This old place?" A tall, nervous-looking woman gripped his arm. "Are you absolutely sure?"

"Absolutely," said Ash. But he felt his cheeks burning. He had never been any good at lying and there was still the big fishy problem of the huge stuffed salmon with the staring eyes.

CHAPTER THIRTY: BEEF WELLINGTON

"Beef Wellington?" Ivy was worried.

Everything had to be perfect for the guests. She had no idea where they had all come from, but it wasn't just the Joneses they had to think about now. There were the new arrivals – the Millers and the Mullers and the Massouds too. And a Madame Moulin from France. As well as a Miss Washington from Sydney, Australia, and a Mr Sydney from Washington, USA. (Not to mention the three elderly McEver sisters, of course.)

To be honest, Ivy was finding it a bit hard to keep up.

It was extraordinary. Ever since Grandpa Digby and the ghosts had gone from Grave Grange, the telephone hadn't stopped ringing and guests just kept turning up. They were fully booked for next week already ... all in spite of the Smiths horrible **STAY-WELL-AWAY.COM** review. Ivy knew it was crazy, but it was almost as if people knew the hotel wasn't haunted any more and they had somehow sensed it was safe to come. But that still left Dad's food to worry about.

"What's wrong with beef Wellington?" he said, opening the oven and grinning as he fanned away great billows of steam. "Beef Wellington's a classic. All the best chefs serve it in their restaurants."

"Really?" Ivy had to admit the warm

meaty odours wafting out of the oven did smell delicious. But you could never be too careful – not with Dad and his experiments. "It's just that beef Wellington sounds a bit ... *rubbery*," she said. "It doesn't have any *actual* wellington boots in it, does it?"

Dad laughed. "Don't be daft! It's just roast beef in crispy pastry," he said. "It's named after a very famous army general – the Duke of Wellington. Not a chewy old welly boot in sight." Then he squeezed Ivy's arm. "Don't worry, love. I've learnt my lesson at long last. I saw the look on Mr and Mrs Smith's faces when I offered them my appetizers. Next thing I knew they were running for their car." He sighed and Ivy saw his shoulders sag as if all the air and excitement had gone out of him. Even his bottom lip was wobbling. "I know my food was to blame..."

"Oh, Dad. It wasn't your fault," said Ivy quickly. (*At least, not entirely*, she thought.) "You mustn't worry about that." She couldn't bear how sad Dad looked. All the same, if he was happy to take a break from pickled eggs in jelly or cabbage and cornflake curry it might be no bad thing.

Once the beef Wellington was ready, she called Ash to help her and they carried the steaming plates of scrumptious-smelling meat and pastry into the dining room and served the guests.

"Delicious!" said Mr Jones.

"Just dandy!" said Mr Sydney.

"Top notch!" agreed Miss Washington.

"*Très bon!*" said Madame Moulin.

Ivy caught sight of Dad peeping through the kitchen door. She gave him a quick thumbs up. Dad just shrugged. Ivy was surprised he didn't look more proud. His perfect main course really was going down a storm.

"How about you?" said Ivy, passing by the McEver sisters' table. "Did you enjoy your beef Wellington?"(Dad had cut theirs up very, very small so that they wouldn't have to chew too much).

"Delightful!" said (probably) Enid.

"Delectable!" said (probably) Ethel.

"Disappointing!" said (probably) Edna, with a cheeky grin. "I thought, knowing your dad, there might be some real wellie boot in it." But she laughed heartily and asked for second helpings all the same.

Everybody seemed to have thoroughly enjoyed the food. Ivy just wished Dad would look more pleased. OK – it wasn't one of his own crazy creations, but the classic dish had been a total success with the diners. Ivy knew she should feel happy

too. This was exactly what she'd wanted –
a busy dining room full of guests all
paying for their dinner. But something was
missing. In spite of all the chatter, Grave
Grange just seemed grey and dull without
the ghosts. *Ordinary!* That was the word
that came to Ivy's mind. It was like serving
Dad's famous tuna–and–marshmallow bake
without the marshmallows. Perfectly nice.
But dull.

Ivy only had to look at Ash's face to
see how much he was missing Misty. She
noticed he kept reaching out as if to stroke
the hound's foggy ears – but there was
nothing there, of course. And she longed
to see Grandpa Digby – they had parted
on such bad terms and there were so many
things she wanted to ask him, stories she
wanted to hear. Perhaps she'd never get the
chance now. She smiled sadly to herself as

she thought what fun the Gory Glove might have had, helping to take down people's orders in the restaurant.

She was being silly, of course. The Gory Glove could never work as a waiter, any more than the phantom Contessa could sing opera in the lounge.

Guests do not like ghosts, she reminded herself. And she thought guiltily of the big spooky salmon, who she had stuffed out of sight behind an umbrella stand in the hall.

When Ivy took the dirty plates back to the kitchen she found Dad had cheered up again. Perhaps he was proud of his beef Wellington  at last. He was leaping around singing Elvis's "All Shook Up" above the sound of the blender as he whisked some strange-looking bright green cream for the pudding.

"That's what it's all about," she muttered to herself, as she went back to the dining room. Dinner really was a great success, and now Dad was dancing for joy. He had found his dream job and was truly happy at last. That could never have happened if the ghosts were still here.

She smiled encouragingly at Ash, who was fidgeting anxiously by the door. She wanted to reassure him everything was going to be all right.

Yet, as Ivy moved between the tables,

asking the guests if they would like any tea or coffee, she noticed that the mood in the dining room seemed to have changed too. Now that the comforting plates of warm beef Wellington were cleared away and finished, it seemed like the guests were waiting for something.

"Pudding will be served shortly," she announced. (She had forgotten to ask Dad what it was. Perhaps that was a mistake. She thought of the bright green cream...)

But nobody seemed particularly interested in dessert.

A very nervous-looking Ms Muller kept glancing out the window. "It's very nearly dark," she said in an excited tone.

Jolly Mr Jones was tapping his foot under the table (quite impatiently, Ivy noticed). "Perhaps they'll appear at long last," he said.

"Who?" asked Ivy. "Are you expecting

more guests … only if you are, I'll have to make up some extra beds."

She glanced at Ash and sighed. They seemed to have done nothing but make beds all day.

"Shh!" said Professor Massoud, taking off her glasses. "I think absolute quiet is best."

"*Mais oui*! *Silence absolu*!" commanded Madam Moulin. She was holding her slender white-gloved hand a few centimetres above her glass of water, gently humming to herself.

They're waiting for something, thought Ivy. *All of them*. But what was it — what were all the guests at Grave Grange waiting for as darkness fell?

She turned to ask Ash in a whisper what he thought it might be. But Ash wasn't there. She caught sight of him running at top speed out of the dining room.

"Wait!" she called. "Where are you going?" But he didn't stop.

"Shh!" hissed the guests.

"Don't make so much noise, pet," said Mrs Jones kindly. "Or the ghosts might never come."

"Ghosts?" Ivy let out a nervous laugh. "I told you, Mrs Jones, there are no ghosts at Grave Grange."

"Don't be silly, my dear," said Professor Massoud. "Of course there are ghosts."

"This spooky old hotel is haunted as sure as I've got a nose on my face," said Mr Sydney.

"We read the review," explained Mrs Miller.

"The one on STAY-WELL-AWAY. COM," agreed Mr Muller.

"You read the review?" Ivy gasped. "All of you?"

Panic was rising in her throat as she looked around the dining room and the guests at every table nodded their heads.

"But it made Grave Grange sound so terrible," said Ivy. "We got minus five stars. If you all read the review, then why on earth are you here?"

"To see the ghosts, of course," said Professor Maussoud.

"*Mais oui, des fantômes*," agreed Madame Moulin.

"We sure can't wait to meet those spooks," said Mr Sydney.

"You mean . . . you *want* to see the ghosts?" said Ivy, as realization began to dawn at last. "You *want* to stay in a haunted hotel?"

"Of course we do, pet," said Mrs Jones, her big pink cheeks glowing with colour. "That silly review by those awful Smith people made it sound so exciting."

"Oh!" Ivy grinned. In a great whoosh she felt her heart fill with bubbling joy (like a cup of Dad's fizzy sherbet tea). "That's wonderful." A huge weight lifted off her shoulders. These guests didn't mind that there were ghosts at Grave Grange. They were pleased. They had come here specially to see the spooks.

Except...

The smile froze on Ivy's lips, her tummy churned and the great weight came crashing back down on to her shoulders like a boulder falling from a cliff.

Except...

There were no ghosts at Grave Grange. Not any more. She had sent them all away. She had banished Grandpa Digby and his spooky friends for nothing.

One thing was certain: she would have to get the ghosts back.

CHAPTER THIRTY-ONE: THE DARK, DARK MOOR

The dark, dark moor spread out beyond Ash in the dark, dark darkness.

Standing at the edge of it, he could see where Darkmoor had got its name from – it was certainly dark. Very dark.

A pale, greenish moon cast strange, eerie shadows across the dark ground, catching a twisted thorn tree here and a hunched rock there.

"Misty!" Ash hollered, jumping at the sound of his own voice. "Misty, are you out there?"

223

Ash's knees were shaking. He longed to turn and run, back to the bright dining room full of chattering guests and to Ivy and Dad, but he had to at least try and see if Misty was still somewhere nearby.

Ash had never had a pet of his own. Even when Ivy had volunteered to bring the class hamster home for the Christmas holidays once, he had refused to let her. Too much scuttling. (And he'd probably have been allergic anyway.) But now that Misty was gone, Ash knew that there were even worse things about having a pet than the sneezing or the scuttling. There was the deep, dark hole of loneliness left behind when the pet was gone.

"Misty!" he called again. "Misty. Can you hear me?"

Maybe she was missing him as much as he was missing her.

But that was foolish. Of course Misty wasn't missing him. She didn't even belong to him. She belonged to (headless) Sir Harold Graves. She was a phantom hound, a proud and ghostly hunting dog, and she had been haunting the rooms of Grave Grange and the hills of Darkmoor for centuries before Ash came along. What use would she have for a silly, scared, skinny boy? The sort of boy who jumped at his own shadow.

Ash whistled (or at least he tried to whistle. He had never been very good at whistling).

"Misty!" he hollered.

He waited for a moment more, counting as slowly as he dared to seventeen inside his head. He was hoping for an answer to his call. He wished he was brave enough to venture on across the moor. But when he was met with only silence and the sound of the wind, he turned and began to run back towards the lighted doorway of the hotel.

"ARH-WOOOOOOOOOOOOOOO-OOOOOO."

A ghostly sound of howling filled the air.

"ARH-WOOOOOOOOOOOOOO-OOOOOOOO."

Ash stopped dead in his tracks. Something was coming closer . . . and closer . . . running towards him from far away across the moors.

"ARH-WOOOOOOOOOOO-OOOOOOOOOO."

"Misty," whispered Ash, hardly daring to turn his head. "Is that you, Misty?"

He really, really hoped it was his beloved ghost hound and not some other terrible creature hurtling straight towards him in the dark.

CHAPTER THIRTY-TWO: A HAUNTING HOWL

A haunting howl echoed through the dining room from somewhere far away across the moors.

ARH-WOOOOOOOOOOOOOO-OOOOOOO.

ARH-WOOOOOOOOOOOOOO-OOOOOOO.

"What was that?" squealed jumpy Ms Muller, leaping up in her seat and spilling her large glass of tomato juice down her white shirt like a pool of blood.

"A hound of hell," cried Mr Sydney. "Sounds like it's coming this way."

"Perhaps a werewolf," said Professor Maussoud, scribbling something in her notebook.

"A ghost of some sort, that's for sure," said Mr Jones, as a cheer went up from all the other guests.

Ivy turned and ran towards the door.

"Please, remain in your seats," she shouted over her shoulder. "Dessert will be served at any moment. It is ... well, I have no idea what it is... but it will a surprise."

Then, before anyone could ask her any questions (either about ghosts or puddings or hounds of hell), she dashed out of the dining room, across the reception hall and over the drawbridge into the dark night.

Ivy paused only to grab three things.

The three things Ivy paused to grab were:

228

One: her coat (it was a cold night).

Two: a candle (it was a dark night).

Three: a box of matches (it was a windy night and the candle was bound to get blown out).

The candle Ivy had chosen was the tallest, brightest one she could see. It was mounted on a large brass candlestick (the big, slightly-dented one that Mirabelle the poltergeist had particularly enjoyed throwing at the wall).

"Ash?" she called out, still managing a gentle jog while keeping the light aflame. "Ash? Are you out here?"

"Over here," came his reply, at the same time as another ghostly howl.

A R H - W O O O O O O O O O O O O - O O O O O O O O.

Ivy held up the candle and saw Ash's slender figure silhouetted against the moon as he stood on the far bank of the murky black pool behind the kitchen bins (the one which she had hoped the Smiths would avoid).

A great dark shape was bounding towards Ash like a demon. Ivy gasped as she saw a huge dog leap towards his neck – then she laughed as it threw its paws across his shoulders and big wet globs of green slobber shone iridescent in the moonlight.

"Misty!" she cried, as the dog ran in wild circles round and round and round Ash's legs, barking and chasing her own tail.

"Hello, old girl," Ash whispered, bending to pat the ghost hound's foggy ears – even from this distance, Ivy could hear a crack in his voice. He cleared his throat and coughed.

"All right. That's quite enough now. Sit!" She saw him bend down and wipe his sticky slobber-covered hands on the stubby grass.

Ivy approached as slowly as she could, giving Ash and Misty time to greet each other, but her own excitement meant she couldn't hold back for long.

"Oh, Ash." She gasped, running up to them both. "Thank goodness Misty's here. Any sign of the other spooks?" She held up the candle and scanned the dark moor behind them. "You'll never guess what, but these guests actually really like—"

"Ghosts," said Ash. For once, it was him finishing her sentence. "I sort of figured that out."

"They read the Smiths' review – all about how Grave Grange might be haunted – and it made them want to come and stay. Isn't it brilliant?" said Ivy. "It means we can fill the hotel rooms with ghost-hunting guests and phantom fanatics galore!"

"Spirit spotters!" Ash laughed.

"Exactly," said Ivy. "The sort of people who want to stay in a run-down, spooky old hotel. The sort of people who like being haunted. Except there's just one problem. . ."

"The ghosts are gone," said Ash, finishing her sentence yet again. "And if there aren't any ghosts, those guests are going to be awfully disappointed. There'll be more bad reviews."

"It's all my fault," said Ivy, crouching down and letting Misty rest her warm foggy head on her shoulder. "I sent Grandpa Digby away. I told him it was either him or us. The other spooks too – I drove them all away."

"Misty came back," said Ash kindly. "So perhaps they all will."

"Do you think so?" Ivy leapt to her feet. "Hello?" she called. "Hello, Grandpa Digby? Are you there?"

There was no reply.

"They could be anywhere," said Ivy, staring into the darkness. She remembered the Gory Glove's note. "Gone hunting? What does that even mean?"

"I don't know," said Ash, as he called out for Grandpa Digby too.

"Mirabelle?" tried Ivy. "Mirabelle,

sweetie-pie, are you there?"

"Sweetie-pie?" Ash sounded like he might choke on his words. "There is nothing sweet about that poltergeist ... even if she is a little girl with ringlets and bows in her hair." He dropped his voice to a whisper. "She's a spoilt-rotten ghost-child, Ivy, and you know it."

"Maybe!" Ivy shrugged. "But I'm fond of her all the same." She called again but there was still no reply. "Sing something," she said, digging Ash in the ribs.

"Sing?" Even in the dark she could feel Ash blush. "No way!"

"Go on! The Contessa might like it," said Ivy, lifting her own voice to the moon. "COME HOME, CONTESSA! OH, CONTESSAAAAA. COME HOOOOOOME."

Ash flat-out refused to join in, and it

was hopeless anyway. The Grave Grange ghosts could be miles away across the moors by now. Grandpa Digby might be so furious with her for driving him out that he would never come back, no matter how hard she looked or how loudly she called.

"I suppose we could get Misty to help us," said Ash quietly. "I mean, she must have been with them when they left. So perhaps she can find them again. She is a hunting dog, after all."

"Ash, you're brilliant," cried Ivy. "We can get Misty to track them and lead us to where they are." She flung her arms around his neck.

"Careful!" Ash yelped. "You'll set me on fire with that candle." But it had gone out anyway.

As she bent down to relight the flame, Ivy suddenly had an idea. "We can use the candlestick to guide Misty's sense of smell," she said, pulling it away from the white, waxy candle and waving the long brass holder under Misty's foggy nose like a bone. "Think how many times Mirabelle used to hurl this candlestick against the wall. Perhaps it's got her scent on it ... if ghosts have a scent."

Ivy had seen a television programme about how the police trained dogs to track down criminals by giving them the scent from something the baddies had owned. It had to be worth a shot.

"Here, girl!" she said, waving the candlestick in the air to entice Misty to sniff it. "Here, girl. Go find Mirabelle. Go find Grandpa Digby."

She threw the long, thin candlestick out into the darkness and waited for Misty to set off on the chase.

CHAPTER THIRTY-THREE: THE MYSTERY OF THE MURKY BLACK POOL

The mystery of the murky black pool had not been revealed for many centuries. Ash wished it could have stayed that way. However, the moment Ivy threw the candlestick in the air, three things happened to change all that:

One: *SPLOSH!* The candlestick landed right in the middle of the murky black pool.

Two: *SPLASH!* Misty dived into the murky black pool to fetch the candlestick back.

Three: *SPLISH!* Misty bounded out of the murky black pool with something in her mouth.

"Good girl!" cheered Ivy, clapping her hands as Misty wagged her tail from side to side with furious pride.

As a beam of moonlight broke through the clouds, Ash tried to speak. He tried to scream. He tried to yell.

But, in the end, all he could do was point.

Misty was not carrying a candlestick in her mouth – she was carrying the long-lost head of Sir Harold Graves.

CHAPTER THIRTY-FOUR: TALLY-HO

"Tally-ho!" cried Headless Harold's dripping wet head. Then its eyes blinked and looked up at Ivy and Ash in surprise. "Who art thou?"

"Hello." Ivy gave a little sort of half curtsey. She wasn't quite sure how to greet a "sir" (especially one who was only a dripping wet, pond-weedy head being held in the jaws of a ghostly hound).

"I'm Ivy," she said. "And this is my twin brother, Ash." (It was obvious Ash was in no fit state to speak for himself.) "I'm the oldest. By twenty-two minutes."

"Bring me my body," cried Sir Harold. "And make haste about it."

"He thinks we're his servants," said Ash in a tiny quivering voice.

"Ah... No, there's been some sort of mix-up, Sir Harold," said Ivy politely. "We're not your servants. We're actually your distant relatives. We're in the Graves family too, you see. You might be our great, great, great ... well, lots and lots of greats ... uncle." She grinned triumphantly. "We're Digby Graves' grandchildren."

She held out the candle so they could both see each other better. It was hard to tell if there was any real family likeness. Sir Harold's head had a massive bristly black beard. But he certainly had Grandpa Digby's bushy eyebrows and the Graves' sticky-out ears.

240

"Relatives? I hate relatives," roared Sir Harold. "Fetch me my body and I'll be done with thee!"

"Right." Ivy could see he wasn't going to be the sort of uncle to sit down on the sofa and share a family photo album with. He didn't look like the sort to remember birthdays, either. Still, it wasn't surprising Sir Harold was a *little* grumpy. After all, his poor head had been lying lost at the bottom of the murky black pool for decades, or maybe even centuries. "The thing is," she said, taking a tiny step backwards, "the whole finding-your-body-thing might be a teeny bit tricky just now. We're not exactly sure where it is. . ."

"Then find it," he roared. "Hunt for it! Send out the hounds."

"Well, we do have *one* hound," said Ivy,

pointing to Misty, who was still clutching Sir Harold's head by the hair. "But we're just not quite sure how to—"

"Silence!" roared Sir Harold as he rolled his eyeballs upwards. "Be this the mangy cur that stole my noggin?"

His head spun round and round like a spinning top as he tried to get a better look at Misty.

The frightened hound shrunk back and her foggy tail drooped between her legs.

"Don't shout at her. She doesn't like it." Ash stepped forward. "Misty did not steal your head, Sir Harold." Ivy could see that his knees were shaking like a bowl of Dad's pickled onion jelly, but he was determined to protect his ghostly pal. "She just found your head in the bottom of the murky pool. It's thanks to Misty that you got out of there at all."

242

But Misty whimpered, dropped Sir Harold's head (which bounced across the ground) and cowered behind Ash's legs.

"Nonsense!" roared Sir Harold's head (still bouncing, until it came to rest against a patch of scrubby heather). "I'd recognize that pesky pooch anywhere. She stole my head from under my arm and ran off with it over two centuries ago now."

"How did it . . . erm, I mean . . . how did your head come off in the first place?" asked Ivy bravely. She didn't like to interrupt Sir Harold's story, but she really was desperate to know.

"Unfortunate accident with a pike," said Sir Harold.

"A pike?" Ivy hardly dared to interrupt again, but she couldn't let it go. "Isn't a pike a kind of fish?"

"Not that kind of pike," roared Sir

Harold. "Nobody has ever had their head knocked off by a fish! It was a sharp pike ... like a spear."

"Ah," said Ivy. "Yes." (She could see that did make more sense.)

"I died in glorious battle, young lady. Not on a trip to the fish market," growled Sir Harold. "Now, where was I, before I was so rudely interrupted..."

"You were dead," said Ivy. "I mean, obviously ... sorry." She felt her cheeks burn. "What I mean is, you were a ghost, carrying your head around under your arm, and Misty here was a ghost too, and..."

"Ah, yes!" Sir Harold's head bellowed. He jutted his chin towards Misty who was still cowering behind Ash's legs. "One fair morn, that ghostly hound gets bored and decides to play fetch with my noggin. Only she didn't play fetch, did she? Because she took off and never brought it back!"

"Misty lost your head!" Ivy gasped. No wonder the poor ghost dog always scurried away when Sir Harold's body materialized through the walls at Grave Grange. She must feel terrible.

"It wasn't Misty's fault," said Ash. "I expect she just forgot where she put it, Sir Harold. She did the same thing with a pair of my socks yesterday..." He trailed off. Ivy could see Ash realizing this wasn't one of his better arguments.

"I'm sure now that Misty's found your head again, she can help find your body too," said Ivy. "After all, she was bred for hunting..."

"Exactly! I bred her myself. I had the finest hunting dogs in all England," boasted Sir Harold. "First sensible thing you've uttered!"

Ivy smiled and gave another little bow.

A plan was coming together in her mind. A brilliant plan. If Sir Harold really could persuade Misty to lead them to wherever his body had gone, then they would find Grandpa Digby and the other spooks too.

"I'm sure you're an excellent huntsman. The very best," she said, smiling down at his head, which was lying like a football in the moonlit heather. "With your wonderful skills to help us find the scent, Misty will have your head back under your arm in no time at all."

"'Tis true!" Sir Harold's head raised a bushy eyebrow as he looked at her. "Perhaps thou art a Graves after all. There's brains in thy noggin, I can tell."

"Well, thank you very much!" said Ivy, with a full-blown curtsey. She couldn't resist turning round and gloating to Ash. "Did you hear that? Brains in my noggin, he said."

"Tally-ho!" cried Sir Harold. "Fetch!"

Misty picked up his head by the hair and carried it in her jaws once more.

"Find!" bellowed Sir Harold.

Misty sniffed the air, then set off at full speed across the moor.

"Come on, Ash," cried Ivy. "We're going on a ghost hunt! We're going to find the Grave Grange ghosts."

CHAPTER THIRTY-FIVE: THE GHOSTLY CHASE

The ghostly chase across the moors was something Ash would never forget.

There were three things which made the hunt so unforgettable (and none of them were good):

One: It was cold.

Two: It was wet.

Three: It was dark.

It was terrifying being dragged across the cold, wet, dark hills of Darkmoor by the screaming head of a (headless) huntsman's ghost.

"Faster!" roared Sir Harold's head. "Faster, you festering ferret-footed children!"

Misty was magnificent. With her nose close to the ground, she never faltered. She stopped only twice – both times to sniff the air, once turning right and once turning left.

At last they entered a small, dark wood.

Every bone in Ash's body wanted to turn around and run. But, as they stumbled down a twisting path between the dark trees, the ghost hound suddenly stopped for a third time and pricked her ears.

"Zounds!" cried Sir Harold's head. "I know this place. My hunting lodge lies yonder."

With a pounding heart, Ash peered into the gloom. Sure enough, as Ivy held up the stubby candle, he could just make out the black shape of a small, dark building through the tangled branches of the gnarled old trees.

"I'm not going in there," protested Ash. "*Nothing* is going to make me go in there!"

"Don't worry," said Ivy. "You'll be fine. We'll all stick together." Ash knew, of course, that the only other choice was to stay out here. Alone. With no candle. Amongst the strange sounds of the eerie wood.

"Fine!" He gulped. "But after that we're going straight home."

Misty led the way towards the tiny tumbledown dwelling. Sir Harold's head was still swinging like a creepy Christmas bauble hanging from her jaws. Ivy followed with the candle barely more than a flicker now.

Ash stuck as close behind her as he could. As he tiptoed forward, he realized he was muttering something under his breath ... and it wasn't his seventeen times table:

"In the dark, dark wood,
there was a dark, dark hut.
In the dark, dark hut,
there was a dark, dark door.
Behind the dark, dark, door
there was a dark, dark room.
And in the dark, dark room,
There were some ..."

CHAPTER THIRTY-SIX: GHOSTS!

"... Ghosts!" cried Ivy in delight.

Cold shadows moved around her as she used the last flicker of the candle to light a dusty iron lamp hanging from the lopsided ceiling of the old hunting lodge. She saw at once that they were all there.

"Hello." She smiled shyly at Grandpa Digby, not sure how he would feel about seeing her. But he floated forward and ruffled her hair with a delighted *ZING!*

"Hello, young nipper!"

Ivy ducked as something long and sharp whizzed past her ear. Mirabelle was idly throwing a quiver full of arrows into a tapestry on the wall as if it was a dartboard.

The Contessa belted-out a greeting in her rich Italian singing voice: "BRAVO BRAAAAVE HUNTERS, FROM THE MIDNIGHT MOOOOOORS."

And the Gory Glove scribbled "Hellow! Wellcome to the hunting lodje," with the end of its finger on a dusty tabletop.

"Hello, everybody!" Ivy smiled. "...And hello, especially, Sir Harold's *body*," she said as the headless huntsman stumbled forward from the shadows and grabbed his head from Misty's jaws.

"Gadzooks! That's better!" he cried, resting the decapitated head snuggly in the crook of his elbow. Then he bent down and gently patted Misty's ears. "Good dog," he said. "Brave hound."

Misty squirmed with delight, then padded back to Ash and sat on his feet.

Ash was still looking utterly terrified, but he managed to smile weakly once Misty was with him again. "Hello, Grandpa Digby," he said. "Hello, ghosts."

Ivy glanced around the tiny hunting lodge. It didn't look as if anyone had been here much since Sir Harold's day. Certainly, if they had, they hadn't done any decorating. It was more like a shack really, with holes in the roof and the roots of trees growing up through the floor. This was a big step down for the mighty ghosts of Grave Grange, who were used to having an endless choice of grand old rooms and echoing passageways to float through.

"I'm so sorry I drove you out of the hotel," she said quietly.

"No. I'm sorry for being such a stubborn old fool," said Grandpa Digby. "I listened to what you said about us spooks wanting someone to haunt, and your guests not wanting to be haunted. I knew you were right: ghosts and guests could never make a go of it at Grave Grange. Then I remembered this old place. I thought we might be able to hole up here for a bit and see if we could find some campers to scare from time to time."

"Hunting!" said Sir Harold brightly.

"No luck though, I'm afraid," said Grandpa Digby. "A big fat waste of time!" Mirabelle stamped her shadowy feet in their pretty little white shoes.

"NOT A DICKIE-BIIIRD," sang the Contessa.

Nufink! scribbled the Gory Glove.

"Not even any day-trippers." Grandpa Digby sighed.

Ivy wasn't surprised. They were in a dark, dark wood on top of dark, dark Darkmoor. If you were to look up "Miles From Anywhere" on a map, you would end up here. It wasn't exactly the sort of place hordes of hikers came flocking to for a nice cream tea and a photo of the view.

"It doesn't matter any more, anyway," she said. "I was wrong. Some guests *do* like ghosts. We've got a whole hotel full of them, waiting for you right now. They're just desperate to be scared silly. I'm sorry, Grandpa Digby. I'm sorry all of you. I was wrong."

"Oh, lass, don't upset yourself," said Grandpa Digby kindly. "As long as we can come home to Grave Grange, that's the main thing."

"You can. You can come tonight," said Ivy, glancing out the window. It was still pitch black outside. "If we hurry, you might even be able to get some decent haunting in before dawn."

"Splendid!" cried Grandpa Digby. "What are we waiting for?" He stepped forward and ruffled Ash and Ivy's hair.

"Brrr!" The pair shivered as usual.

The Gory Glove kicked dust in the air and did a little jig on the tippy-tips of its fingers.

"Tally-ho!" cheered Sir Harold.

The Contessa banged on the table for silence and then sang a slow and rather-moving song called "HOMEWARD BOUND!" It made Misty howl like a wolf.

"Lead on then, lass," said Grandpa, smiling at Ivy and gesturing to the door once the singing was done.

But one ghost was not happy.

"No!" screamed a furious voice. "I'm not going anywhere! I shan't, shan't, shan't!"

Ivy ducked just in time as a fresh flurry of real arrows – with very sharp ends – flew past her head.

THWACK! THWACK! THWACK!

They landed in the door.

"I'm going to stay right here," sulked Mirabelle, stamping her foot again.

Ivy was tempted to ignore her. She was tempted to set off anyway and hope that Mirabelle followed. But she knew she couldn't do that. Mirabelle was only a very little ghost after all.

"You told us to go away, now you say we have to come back. I don't like you! You're bossy," whined Mirabelle, sticking her (ghostly-blue) tongue out at Ivy and blowing a huge raspberry.

"Well. . ." Ivy was thinking fast. But it was Ash who stepped forward and saved the day (perhaps because he was desperate to get out of the creepy shack as fast as he possibly could).

"How about if we make it worth your while to come back with us?" he said. "There must be something that you want?"

"You mean a present?" Mirabelle screeched with joy. "Yes! Yes! Yes! I want a present! I do."

"Brilliant!" Ivy gave Ash a quick thumbs up. She should have known a spoilt spook like Mirabelle would be open to bribes.

"What do you want us to get you? You can have anything you like," she said.

"Let me see now. . ." Mirabelle began to twirl her ringlet-y hair between her fingers. "Hmmm!"

"I WANT SOMETHING NICE

TOOOOO," sang the Contessa. "OR I
SHALL NOT COMEEEE EITHER."

"Fine!" said Ivy. "You can all have
something. What would you like, Contessa?"

"I WANT A PUUUUUDDING," she
sang.

"A pudding?" Ivy smiled. Well, that was
easy. "I'll get Dad to make you a delicious
dessert as soon as we get home," she said.

"I DON'T WANT TO EAT ONEEEE!"
trilled the Contessa.

"Ghosts can't eat anything. Not a morsel,"
Grandpa Digby explained.

"Ah!" said Ivy (at least that answered that
question; she'd been wondering for a while).

"It's a rotten pity." Grandpa Digby sighed.
"I'd sell my eternal soul for a grape and
gherkin sandwich with extra jam and chilli
sauce."

Ivy giggled. (That explained where Dad

had inherited his peculiar taste in food, at least.)

"But if you can't eat, then why do you want a pudding?" she asked the Contessa.

"I DON'T WANT TO EAT A PUUUUDDING, I WANT A PUUUUDDING TO HAVE MY NAME!" trilled the Contessa – then she blew out her cheeks as if she was utterly fed up with singing and started to speak in a soft English country voice, which took Ivy quite by surprise.

"T'aint fair. That Dame Nellie Melba, she were an opera singer like me and they named Peach Melba pudding after her. Proper lovely, it is. Ice cream and peaches – soft as you like. And that swirly, twirly Anna Pavlova what were a ballet dancer, she got Pavlova pudding. Scrumptious it is. All white meringue and cream. You ain't anybody really until you've had a pudding what's got your name."

"Oh!" said Ivy. She'd had a Pavlova once. It was delicious – but she hadn't realized these puddings were named after famous performers from the past. (*Sounds a bit like beef Wellington and that old army general*, she thought. *What was it about dead people trying to get themselves remembered on menus? Still, if it was good enough for old General Welly-boot, it was good enough for their phantom opera singer too.*)

"You shall have a pudding of your own, Contessa, I promise," she said. "A wonderful one! I'll ask Dad to name a dessert especially for you and we'll put it on the hotel menu in your honour. People will come from miles around just to eat a Contessa Custard or a ... what's your surname, Contessa?

"SHUFFLEBOTTOM," she sang. "DOTTY SHUFFLEBOOOOTTOOOOM."

Ivy tired her very best not to laugh. "Maybe a stunning Shufflebottom Soufflé?" she said. "Or a delicious Dotty Dumpling? I'll get it all arranged as soon as we get back to Grave Grange. Now ... does anybody else want anything before we leave?"

New qwill penne? scribbled the Gory Glove.

"Of course," said Ivy. That seemed reasonable enough.

"I desire only to hang on to my precious noggin'," said Sir Harold wisely, tucking his head tightly under his elbow and glaring at Misty over the top of his sleeve.

"I'm just pleased to be coming home with my grandchildren who I'll have the chance to get to know," said Grandpa Digby happily.

Ivy grinned, though she suddenly felt a tear in the corner of her eye and had to blink. "Thank you," she whispered. "I can't wait either."

"Nor me!" said Ash

Misty wagged her tail, which Ivy guessed meant something similar.

"Well that's it, then," she said. "We're all sorted. Shall we go?"

Unfortunately, she had forgotten that the young poltergeist had not yet made up her mind.

"Wait!" Mirabelle flew across the ceiling, cackling with delight. "I know what I want!" she screeched. "I want a pony!"

CHAPTER THIRTY-SEVEN: THE WAY HOME

The way home over the moors was even worse than the journey to the hunting lodge had been.

There were three reasons why Ash found it even more terrible (and none of them were good reasons).

One: It was colder than before.

Two: It was wetter than before.

Three: It was darker than before.

Worse still, Mirabelle kept throwing stones and whining about when she was going to get the pony she'd been promised.

"I want a Darkmoor pony," she said. "A really cute one!"

"Keep your eyes peeled," said Ivy. "You might spot one out on the moors if you're lucky."

"Probably galloping around with no head," muttered Ash, but he was surprised to feel his spirits soar as he saw the pale lights of Grave Grange over the hill.

Even Mirabelle stopped whining.

"Now listen up, everybody," said Grandpa Digby. "We're going to go in there and have some fun. We'll scare those guests silly. Mind you don't hover around too long, though."

"Just a glimpse," agreed Sir Harold.

"A SPOOOOOKY SERENADE," sang the Contessa (her Italian accent back again, although they all knew now she was really Dotty Shufflebottom).

"And, Mirabelle," warned Grandpa Digby, "don't actually hit anyone when you're throwing things around."

"Aw!" Mirabelle looked like she was about to have another fit.

"You'd better get going," said Ash quickly, before she could erupt.

"Happy haunting!" cheered Ivy.

"And don't scare anyone *too* much," said Ash.

Most of the ghosts had already vanished inside. But Grandpa Digby turned and looked back at them. "Aren't you two nippers coming in to see the fun?" he asked.

Ash shook his head. He'd had almost more than he could take for one night. "I think I'll stay out here a minute more," he said. "I'm just going to catch my breath."

Misty lay down by his feet, but he was surprised when Ivy said that she'd stay too.

"Suit yourselves," said Grandpa Digby. "I'll see you later on. We've got a lot of catching up to do, young nippers."

With that he slid through a tiny gap in the lounge window and vanished like smoke.

"Listen," said Ash. "I can hear singing."

It wasn't the Contessa (not yet).

Ash held up a hand to Misty. "Stay!" he said, and she lay down obediently on the grass.

Then he and Ivy crept round the corner of the building and saw Dad dancing in the moonlight as he belted out an Elvis tune and emptied a bucket of kitchen scraps into the compost bin behind the murky black pool.

"Hello, you two." He smiled, looking up and seeing

them. "You come out for a breath of fresh air?"

"Something like that," said Ash.

"Have you had a good evening feeding all those guests?" asked Ivy. "Are you enjoying it here?"

"I'm loving it," said Dad and his face lit up. "I know they liked the beef Wellington. That's a classic. But I think it was my pudding which was the real hit."

"Really?" said Ash. "What was it, exactly?"

"A thick spongy bottom, with wobbly pink jelly on top," said Dad.

So far, so good, thought Ash. "It sounds a bit like a trifle."

"Ah, yes, but here's the fun bit." Dad beamed. "Instead of custard, I added a layer of curry sauce. Then I topped the whole lot off with a lovely green bean cream."

"Right!" said Ash, feeling a little

queasy. "Good to see you haven't lost your experimental streak."

"And what did you call this wonderful wobbly pud?" asked Ivy, catching Ash's eye.

"That's just the thing," said Dad. "I can't decide."

"Call it the Dotty Shufflebottom," said Ivy and Ash at exactly the same time.

"Hmmm. The *Dotty Shufflebottom*?" said Dad. "Yes, I like that."

He picked up the empty scraps bucket and turned to go back inside.

"Dotty Shufflebottom," whispered Ivy. "The Contessa will be over the moon."

"A Grave Grange special!" Ash laughed.

But Dad stopped suddenly in the kitchen doorway and spun around.

"What's that?" he said, pointing towards the murky pool. "Over there? I thought I saw something drinking from the pond?"

Ash stared through the darkness. His heart was pounding. What new terrible thing could be lurking out there on the moors?

"Look," said Ivy, grabbing his sleeve. "It's a little pony. A Darkmoor pony."

"Isn't it cute," said Dad and he carried on inside, singing another Elvis song under his breath.

It was only after Dad's back was turned that the shaggy creature lifted its head and looked up at them across the water. It had bright red, glowing eyes and fire burning in its nostrils.

"Adorable," said Ash with a shudder. At least it had a head. "Mirabelle will be thrilled."

A moment later there was a sudden sound from inside the hotel. The Darkmoor pony reared up on its hind legs and galloped away into the night.

The sound which had startled the red-eyed beast was a scream. A human scream ... as if someone inside the building had just seen a ghost.

This was followed by a second scream and then a third.

There was a loud crash, as if a china plate had been thrown. Then another scream as the sound of distant, eerie opera singing wafted through the night air.

Misty, who had bounded back to Ash's heel, raised her head and howled like a wolf.

"Look!" said Ash. He saw Grandpa Digby's shadowy shape wafting past an upstairs window. The old ghost stopped for a moment and gave them a quick spooky thumbs up.

"Brilliant!" said Ivy.

"Excellent!" agreed Ash.

Everything was going to plan.

The guests at Grave Grange were having a perfectly scary time.

FIVE STAR REVIEW

WWW.HAUNTEDHOLS.COM

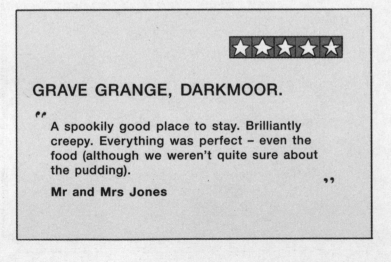

★★★★★

GRAVE GRANGE, DARKMOOR.

"
A spookily good place to stay. Brilliantly creepy. Everything was perfect – even the food (although we weren't quite sure about the pudding).
"

Mr and Mrs Jones

A SALES PITCH

Dont bye this sillie booke by Loo
Kuefvzlerrr (I'm not even going
to try and speel that). Bye mine.
Its muche bettre.

The Trooo Storie ov Grave Grange by the Gory Glove

(With realley woobbly speelling.)

ANOTHER SALES PITCH

END NOTE:
SOMETHING FISHY

Something fishy was lurking, forgotten, behind the umbrella stand in the Reception Hall.

Typical! thought the stuffed salmon. *Why do they always forget about me?*

ACKNOWLEDGEMENTS

It is SPOOKY how much incredible help
I have had with this book! Huge thank
you's to: Claire Wilson and Miriam
Tobin at RCW, my wonderful editor
Eishar Brar, eagle-eyed Pete Matthews,
Steve Brown for his fabulous cover
and illustrations and Bethany Mincher
for design. Also Lauren Molyneux and
Bethan Chaplin-Dewey in Sales and
Marketing and all the bone-rattlingly
brilliant team at Scholastic.